"I should go." Common sense dictated that Isla should leave but her feet refused to move. She should have run back to the villa the moment she spotted Andreas on the beach, Isla thought ruefully. Instead she had walked toward him, forgetting her loyalty to Stelios, compelled by a force, a need that was beyond her control.

The truth was she was fascinated by him, and she swallowed audibly when he lifted his hand and smoothed a few damp strands of her hair off her face.

"Stay until the storm has passed." His voice was a low growl.

Isla wasn't sure if he meant the storm outside or the one that had simmered between them since they had been on the island. When he slowly lowered his head toward her, she couldn't move, could hardly breathe. She wanted him to kiss her. There was no point pretending otherwise.

Chantelle Shaw lives on the Kent coast and thinks up her stories while walking on the beach. She has been married for over thirty years and has six children. Her love affair with reading and writing Harlequin stories began as a teenager, and her first book was published in 2006. She likes strong-willed, slightly unusual characters. Chantelle also loves gardening, walking and wine!

Books by Chantelle Shaw

Harlequin Presents

Acquired by Her Greek Boss
Hired for Romano's Pleasure
The Virgin's Sicilian Protector
Reunited by a Shock Pregnancy
Wed for the Spaniard's Redemption

Secret Heirs of Billionaires

Wed for His Secret Heir

Wedlocked!

Trapped by Vialli's Vows

Bought by the Brazilian

Mistress of His Revenge
Master of Her Innocence

The Saunderson Legacy

The Secret He Must Claim
The Throne He Must Take

Visit the Author Profile page
at Harlequin.com for more titles.

Chantelle Shaw

PROOF OF THEIR
FORBIDDEN NIGHT

Recycling programs
for this product may
not exist in your area.

ISBN-13: 978-1-335-14835-3

Proof of Their Forbidden Night

Copyright © 2020 by Chantelle Shaw

For questions and comments about the quality of this book,
please contact us at CustomerService@Harlequin.com.

Harlequin Enterprises ULC
22 Adelaide St. West, 40th Floor
Toronto, Ontario M5H 4E3, Canada
www.Harlequin.com

Printed in U.S.A.

PROOF OF THEIR
FORBIDDEN NIGHT

CHAPTER ONE

'WHAT DO YOU think of the news that Papa is engaged to the Ice Queen? Isla has hooked her claws into him, make no mistake.'

Andreas Karelis came to an abrupt halt a few feet away from the helicopter which had brought him to his family's privately owned island, Louloudi, and stared at his sister, who had run across the garden to meet him. Nefeli's shrilly furious voice had risen above the *whomp-whomp* of the slowing rotor blades.

From the air the island, partially covered with a cedar forest and olive groves, resembled an emerald set amid the azure Aegean Sea. Andreas's happiest boyhood memories were of running free on Louloudi, away from his parents' expectations of the Karelis heir. He owned houses in California and the French Riviera and a penthouse apartment in Athens, but Louloudi was the only place he thought of as home.

'I have heard nothing from Stelios,' he said curtly and his sister's eyes widened. Usually Andreas kept a tight control over his feelings and no one, not even

Nefeli, who was the only person he was at all close to, knew what he was thinking. But he disliked surprises, good or bad, and this was definitely the latter.

'I thought Papa might have phoned you. He dropped the bombshell when I arrived.' Nefeli tossed her dark curls over her shoulders. She was petite with a volatile temperament—the opposite of Andreas, who owed his tall, athletic build to his Californian maternal grandmother and had learned early in his childhood to suppress his emotions. It was a lesson he had mastered with astonishing success.

'A press statement will be released tomorrow to formally announce Papa's engagement to Isla, but he wanted to share the news with his family first. God!' Nefeli's voice went up another octave. 'She's his housekeeper, and young enough to be his daughter. What is Papa *thinking*?'

Andreas gave a careless shrug to hide his violent dislike of his father's matrimonial plans. The strength of his reaction surprised him, and he reminded himself that Stelios was free to do as he pleased. There was no fool like an old fool, especially a widowed, elderly billionaire in thrall to a beautiful young woman, he thought sardonically.

A restlessness gripped him as he visualised the woman who was now apparently Stelios's fiancée. Isla Stanford was undeniably beautiful. An English rose with her spun-gold hair and creamy skin. But she had an untouchable air that Andreas would usually find off-putting. He preferred women who were sexually confident, which was why he had found his intense awareness of Isla on the few occasions that he had met her so puzzling.

'Papa has brought her to Louloudi and she is to attend my birthday party at the weekend,' Nefeli said sulkily. She slipped her hand through her brother's arm as they walked towards the villa. 'You will have to do something, Andreas.'

'What do you suggest?' His trademark lazy drawl with its blend of cynical amusement disguised his thoughts but his restless feeling intensified when Nefeli spoke again.

'Why don't you seduce her? I'm sure you could quite easily. Women always fall at your feet, and when Papa realises that the Ice Queen had only pretended to be interested in him for his money, he'll get rid of her and everything will return to normal.'

By *normal* Nefeli presumably meant that Stelios would revert to behaving like a man in his late sixties who should be preparing for his retirement instead of lusting after a blonde bimbo who saw cash signs when she looked at him. Except that Isla was not your average bimbo. It would make life a lot easier if she was, Andreas brooded.

'I don't want to risk getting frostbite,' he quipped. He swore silently. It wasn't that he had any objection to his father taking another wife. Just not *her*. Not Isla. Why couldn't the old man marry a woman of a similar age to him? A comfortably plump widow who would share Stelios's twilight years, rather than an ice-cool blonde with intelligent grey eyes and a Mona Lisa smile that drove Andreas to distraction.

His thoughts flew back to eighteen months ago when he had been summoned to the house in Kensington which his father had purchased shortly after his wife's death, some six months earlier. Stelios's decision to move to London had been a surprise, and after Andreas had handed his rain-spattered jacket to the butler and been shown into the drawing room, he'd intended to ask why his father had chosen to live in a country with such an infernal climate.

But his mind went blank and his gaze was riveted on the woman sitting close to Stelios on the sofa. Too damned close, had been Andreas's first thought, followed by a strong urge to snatch her away from his father's side. She rose to her feet, as graceful and supple as a ballerina, and slipped her hand beneath Stelios's arm when he stood up. Her solicitousness as she hovered protectively next to his father had irked Andreas.

'Andreas, finally you have found the time to pay me a visit.'

Stelios's greeting held a note of criticism which Andreas had come to expect, and he gritted his teeth as he stepped forwards to kiss his father's cheek. 'It is good to see you looking well, Papa.'

In fact his father looked tired, but Andreas barely noticed and his attention was on the woman. Who was she? Stelios's personal assistant perhaps? Her appearance gave no clue to her role in Stelios's life. She was wearing a white dress with three-quarter-length sleeves and a softly flared skirt that fell to just below her knees. A narrow black belt around her slender waist and black patent stiletto-heeled shoes were elegant accessories. Her hair was the colour of pale honey, drawn back from her face and tied in a ponytail that reached halfway down her back. She looked as demure as a nun, but the curve of her full lips and her high, firm breasts suggested an understated sensuality.

Andreas couldn't take his eyes off her and he gave a jolt when his father said drily, 'Allow me to introduce my housekeeper, Miss Stanford. Isla, this is my son, Andreas.'

'I'm pleased to meet you,' she murmured.

Her voice made Andreas think of a cool mountain stream and at that precise moment he would have gladly jumped into an ice bath to put out the fire raging inside him.

'The pleasure is mine, Miss Stanford.' He had intended to sound sardonic, but the word *pleasure* hovered in the air, infusing his greeting with sensual heat and something that sounded to his own ears like a challenge. He noticed the faint flush of rose pink that stained her cheeks like the sweep of an artist's brush over a white canvas. Her eyes widened a fraction and Andreas glimpsed his confusion mirrored in those grey depths. There was another emotion too. He recognised a flash of awareness, before her long eyelashes that were a few shades darker than her hair swept down and shut him out. Time juddered to a standstill. In the silence Andreas heard the harsh rasp of his breath and the unevenness of hers, but when she met his gaze again her expression was unreadable.

She turned to Stelios. 'I'll go and make tea.'

'Thank you, my dear.' A look passed between the old man and his housekeeper that Andreas could not decipher. Irritation swept through him. When the hell had his father, a lifelong coffee addict, started drinking tea?

'I prefer coffee,' he said abruptly, earning a frown from Stelios.

'Of course.' Isla Stanford gave a perfunctory smile that made Andreas long to ruffle her composure. He wanted, badly, to discover if there was heat beneath her ice and if her lips would fit the shape of his as perfectly as he imagined.

She stepped past him and her elusive perfume teased his senses. He watched the sway of her hips as she walked across the room and heard himself blurt out, 'Would you like some help?'

'I can manage, thank you.' She sounded amused. Pausing in the doorway, she glanced back at him and her brows arched as she gave him a speculative look that made him feel like a wet-behind-the-ears schoolboy. 'Or don't you trust that I can make Greek coffee, Andreas?'

The way she spoke his name in her soft English accent had made him want to growl like a predatory beast.

Andreas hadn't trusted *her,* and every time he had met Isla on subsequent visits to his father in London his instincts warned him that she was trouble. Now the news of Stelios's engagement to the woman his sister had christened the Ice Queen proved that those instincts had been right.

He followed Nefeli into the house, where the marble-lined entrance hall was blessedly cool after the heat outside. Andreas had left California sixteen hours ago. Admittedly, travelling by private jet was not arduous but he was looking forward to a leisurely shower and a drink. He was about to ask the butler Dinos to bring a whisky and soda to his room when his sister turned to him.

'You had better hurry up and get changed. You're later than expected. Papa has arranged a formal dinner party this evening to celebrate his engagement to Isla.' She grimaced. 'I can't believe he is planning to marry her. He's making a fool of himself. Can't you think of *anything* that might make Papa see sense?'

Nefeli's plea stayed in Andreas's mind when he entered his private suite of rooms and quickly showered, before he donned black suit trousers, a snowy white shirt and a black dinner jacket. He would have preferred to pull on a pair of old denim shorts and a T-shirt and stroll down to the beach, but instead he had to sit through a dinner party to mark his father's betrothal. *Theos!* He glowered at his reflection in the mirror and raked his fingers through his unruly dark hair that moments ago he'd attempted to tame with a comb.

He could in fact think of something that might make his father question his relationship with his erstwhile housekeeper who was now his fiancée. What if he were to reveal how Isla had come apart in his arms when he'd kissed her in London a month ago? Would Stelios be so keen to marry her?

Andreas's jaw clenched at the memory of Isla's wild response to him—the way she had opened her mouth beneath his and made a husky moan when he'd thrust his tongue between her lips. With a frown he acknowledged that he had kissed Isla to satisfy his curiosity, but she had tested his control in a way he hadn't expected. So much so that he had cut his trip to England short and flown back to California the next day.

Had Isla set her sights on a bigger prize? Stelios was the head of Karelis Corp—the family-owned business which operated the largest oil refinery in Europe. The company also ran the biggest chain of fuel stations in Greece and had interests in shipping and banking. Andreas was the heir to the Karelis business empire but he was in no rush to take over from his father. He had carved out a career as a champion rider in the World Superbike league until a serious accident had forced him to retire from motorbike racing.

Forcing his thoughts back to the present, Andreas muttered a curse and strode out of his suite. He paused in the corridor outside his father's private apartment and knocked on the door. If he could have a conversation with Stelios and his new fiancée before dinner, he might have a clearer understanding of the reason for their surprise engagement. There was no reply, and after waiting for a few seconds he opened the door and glanced around the sitting room. The door leading to the bedroom was closed and the idea that Stelios was in there with Isla evoked a corrosive feeling in the pit of Andreas's stomach.

The bedroom door opened and, before he had time to retreat, the butler walked through to the sitting room. 'I thought that my father and Miss Stanford might be here,' Andreas explained.

'Kyrios Stelios is downstairs in the salon. He asked me to fetch his glasses.' Dinos lifted his hand, in which he held a spectacles case. 'Miss Stanford's room is next door but she is down in the salon with your father.'

So Stelios and Isla were not sharing a bedroom at the villa, Andreas mused as he descended the marble staircase. It struck him as unusual behaviour for a couple who had announced their intention to marry. The whole situation of the sudden engagement was odd, especially as his father hadn't mentioned his marriage plans at their last meeting a month ago.

It was not his concern if Stelios made a fool of himself over his pretty young housekeeper, Andreas told himself. If he admitted that passion had flared between him and Isla, his father might not believe him, or might accuse him of trying to make trouble. Their relationship had never been close, especially after Stelios had been forced to choose between his wife and family, and his mistress.

Andreas had been twelve when his father had admitted that he'd been seeing another woman in England and intended to leave his marriage for her. Andreas's mother had been devastated, and Andreas had vowed that he would never speak to his father again unless he dumped his mistress and returned to his wife and children. He'd hoped that by taking his mother's side he would win her love, but she had continued to treat him with the same disinterest that she'd always shown him. His father had remained married but from then on he had been cool towards Andreas.

Helia Karelis had died two years ago from an overdose of her sleeping pills. A tragic accident, the coroner had recorded, but Andreas was sure his mother had known what she was doing when she'd swallowed a handful of pills, just as he was sure she had never got over her husband's affair, even though it had happened many years ago. Her unhappiness with her marriage had proved to Andreas the folly of falling in love. He avoided emotional dramas in the same way that any sane person would take precautionary measures against coming into contact with the Ebola virus.

As for Isla, Andreas shrugged his shoulders. He couldn't explain why he had come on to her like a teenager on a first date in London. It wasn't his style and he was confident that when he met her again he would see her for the gold-digger he suspected she was. The way she had responded to his kiss with a sweet ardency that had almost made him believe she was inexperienced must have been an act, he told himself.

He strode into the salon where pre-dinner cocktails were being served and stopped dead in his tracks. The room was full of guests—various relatives and, curiously, considering the dinner party was supposed to be a family gathering, several high-ranking representatives from the oil industry were present as well as members of Karelis Corp's board of directors. There was a low hum of chatter, the clink of glasses on silver trays carried by the serving staff. But Andreas only saw Isla and his blood thundered in his ears.

This was a different Isla to the decorous housekeeper he had met on previous occasions at his father's house in Kensington. Tonight she was a lady in red—a sultry siren in clingy scarlet velvet, with sparkling jewels around her throat that drew his attention to the pale upper slopes of her breasts above the plunging neckline of her dress. Her blonde hair was swept up into a chignon to expose the delicate line of her neck. The scarlet gloss on her lips emphasised their fullness.

Lowering his gaze, he saw that the hem of her dress came to her mid-thigh and her long slim legs were enhanced by high-heeled strappy shoes. Isla Stanford was every hot-blooded male's fantasy and Andreas was burning up. She looked over at him, and as their eyes locked he saw a pink stain spread across her face.

The convulsive movement of her throat when she swallowed told him that she was as aware as he was of the electrical current that arced between them. He stared at her mouth, so lush and red and infinitely inviting, and felt the urgent stirring of his desire swell beneath his trousers.

For a moment Andreas forgot that Isla was attending the party as Stelios's guest. Something primitively possessive swept through him and he strode across the room, driven to stake his claim on the woman who had been in his thoughts too often in the past months. He and Isla had unfinished business.

But just then his father finished talking to another guest and slipped his arm around Isla's waist. Andreas's eyes narrowed as he halted in front of the mismatched couple.

'Finally, you are here.' Stelios sounded irritable. 'I expected you to arrive several hours ago. We were about to start dinner without you.'

'Good evening, Papa,' Andreas greeted his father drily. 'Miss Stanford.' He kept his expression bland as he glanced at Isla and back to Stelios. 'I apologise if I am late. I said I would arrive some time in the afternoon but I did not specify an exact time and I was unaware that you were giving a dinner party.'

Stelios sniffed. 'Well, you are here now. I hope you will offer your congratulations when I tell you that Isla has agreed to be my fiancée.'

Even though Andreas had been pre-warned by his

sister of his father's engagement, the sight of a diamond the size of a rock on Isla's finger filled him with fury. It had to be a joke, surely? This grey-haired, wrinkled old man and an exquisite English rose who must be some forty years younger than her future husband.

He jerked his gaze to Isla's face and noted the faint quiver of her lower lip, the flash of sexual awareness in her wide grey eyes that she quickly concealed beneath the sweep of her lashes. She was *his*, goddammit. Yet it was his ageing father's arm around her slender waist and Stelios's obscenely gaudy ring glittering on her finger.

'Well, Andreas?' his father prompted. 'I can see you are surprised by my news, but I'm sure you will agree that I am a lucky man to have such a beautiful fiancée.'

At a rough guess, the diamond solitaire was worth a six-figure sum. Andreas gave a sardonic smile. 'Congratulations,' he drawled, directing his mocking gaze at Isla. 'You appear to have hit the jackpot.'

CHAPTER TWO

THE INSOLENCE OF the man! Isla's temper had simmered throughout the interminable five-course dinner as Andreas's loaded comment echoed in her ears. Thankfully, he had sat at the far end of the table from where she and Stelios were seated, but she'd felt his brilliant blue eyes watching her, and his speculative gaze added to her tension in a situation that was already uncomfortable.

From halfway down the table, she'd been aware of the poisonous looks that Stelios's daughter directed at her. At the end of the dinner, Stelios had stood up and asked the guests to raise their glasses in a toast to his new fiancée. It was taking the pretence too far and Isla's doubts about what she was doing on Louloudi had intensified.

Giving a soft sigh, she pushed open the French windows and stepped outside onto the terrace. It was dark now, and the stunning view across the gardens to the sea beyond was hidden. Although summer was coming to an end, the night was sultry and the air was thick with the scents of rosemary and lavender which grew in big terracotta pots.

Isla's hand strayed to the ruby and diamond necklace around her throat and once again she checked that the clasp was securely fastened.

'I'm terrified I might lose it,' she'd whispered to Stelios earlier in the day while they had posed for photographers in the boardroom of Karelis Corp in Athens. 'The necklace must be worth a fortune. I'd feel happier wearing something less ostentatious.'

Stelios had dismissed her concerns and taken hold of her hand, lifting it up to brush his lips across the enormous diamond ring that he'd slipped onto her finger just before they had faced the cameras. 'Try to relax and smile,' he murmured. 'The eyes of the world will be on you when the news of our betrothal is announced in the media tomorrow. I am a billionaire and people will expect my fiancée to wear fabulous jewellery and dress in haute couture.'

After the press conference recording they had boarded a helicopter for the short flight to Stelios's island. When they were seated in the helicopter's luxurious cabin he gave her a wry smile. 'I'm sure I don't need to remind you of the importance of making our engagement appear convincing in front of the press. It is vital at this time of financial turbulence that Karelis Corp's competitors believe I am a strong leader of the company. Just as importantly, I want to hide my illness from my family until after my daughter's twenty-first birthday.'

'I know you are trying to protect Nefeli. But I urge you to tell her and Andreas the truth. Your children won't be pleased about our engagement. They already dislike me.'

Stelios's daughter had barely hidden her hostility towards Isla whenever she had visited her father at his home in Kensington. And Andreas had nothing but disdain for her. Isla was quite certain of that, even though she had only met him a handful of times. Oh, on the surface he was polite enough. Quite charming, in fact. But she wasn't fooled by his laid-back air and the careless smile that curved his lips but did not match the coldly cynical expression in his eyes.

She didn't know why Andreas had disapproved of her when she'd been employed as his father's housekeeper, or why he'd kissed her the last time he had come to London. The kiss had been unexpected, which was why she had responded to him, she assured herself.

'You are mistaken. I am sure my children find you delightful.' Stelios had sought to reassure her. 'I need you to be the focus of attention. Everyone will be fascinated by my beautiful fiancée and they won't notice that I have lost weight. I will explain about my illness when the time is right to do so. But I want Nefeli to enjoy her twenty-first birthday party, spared from the knowledge that I will not be around to celebrate future birthdays with her.'

Isla couldn't argue with Stelios's reasoning or his desire to protect his daughter when she understood the devastation of losing a parent. It had taken her a long time to come to terms with her mum's death in a horrific accident. Tragically, Stelios had arrived in England in search of Marion six months too late.

The muted sounds of the party drifted across the terrace and Isla was glad to be outside, away from the spotlight for a few minutes. The ruby necklace felt heavy around her neck and she wished she hadn't allowed Stelios to persuade her to wear it. But he had insisted that the necklace and matching drop earrings were perfect accessories for the red dress he'd suggested she should wear to the press conference and dinner party. The tight-fitting dress clung to her body and the scooped neckline revealed more of her cleavage than Isla was comfortable with. She did not normally wear attention-grabbing clothes. But the point of her overtly sexy outfit and the reason for the announcement of their engagement was to draw attention away from Stelios's ill-health.

The sound of footsteps on the terrace behind her caused the hairs on the back of her neck to stand on end, a sixth sense warning her of imminent danger. She froze when a mocking voice drawled, 'Ah, the blushing bride-to-be! You *have* been a clever girl, Isla.'

Her heart gave an annoying flip, as it always did when Stelios's son was in the vicinity, and it took every ounce of her willpower to turn towards him when her instincts urged her to flee. Somehow she managed to say calmly, 'Whatever do you mean, Andreas?'

The simple act of uttering his name evoked a wild heat inside her, and she prayed he would think her cheeks were flushed because the temperature in Greece was much warmer than the chilly, grey England she had left two days ago. Isla hated that Andreas Karelis made her feel like a gauche teenager but she suspected he had the same effect on most women.

Handsome did not come near to describing his sculpted features, with those razor-edge cheekbones, square jaw and outrageously sensual mouth that looked as if it had been shaped entirely for the purpose of kissing. His hair was the same shade of dark brown as the rich Greek coffee she had served him when he had visited his father at the house in Kensington.

It was not just his height—she estimated that he was three or four inches over six foot—or his attractive features, dominated by his startling blue eyes, that set him apart from other men. Andreas possessed a smouldering sensuality that Isla could not ignore, however much she wished she could.

Although he had retired from motorbike racing he was still regarded as a sporting legend by an army of adoring groupies. His reputation as a playboy was reinforced by stories of his love-life played out in the pages of tabloid newspapers and celebrity gossip magazines. Not that Isla took the slightest interest in the scandalous headlines about Andreas, but she knew they upset his father and she had resolved to protect Stelios from stress and worry as much as she possibly could for the time he had left.

It was inexplicable the way her pulse quickened and her breasts rose and fell jerkily when she was anywhere near Andreas. Worse was the realisation that he knew the effect he had on her. He smiled, baring his teeth and reminding her of a wolf that had cornered its prey. Isla considered walking as quickly as her skyscraper stiletto heels would permit, back inside the villa where Stelios was chatting with some of his dinner guests. But before she could move Andreas stepped towards her and she found herself edging up against the stone balustrade.

In the moonlight he seemed even bigger and distinctly menacing as his muscular, whipcord body loomed over her. There was nothing she could do but brazen it out and she forced herself to tilt her head and meet his hard stare.

'I have a feeling that you were not paying me a compliment when you called me clever,' she remarked, pleased that she sounded composed when she felt anything but.

His eyes narrowed, but not before she'd glimpsed a flash of surprise at her challenging tone. 'There are words to describe women like you and none of them are complimentary.'

Isla blinked, taken aback by the ferocity in Andreas's low voice. The contemptuous curl of his lips caused a stab of hurt beneath her breastbone. Her treacherous heart hammered when he lifted his hand and ran his forefinger over the rubies at her throat.

'Very pretty,' he said, still in that harsh tone that seemed to come from deep within him. But although he touched the blood-red stones strung alternately between sparkling diamonds, his eyes were on her face and his expression made her shiver and burn simultaneously. She held her breath when he moved his hand up to one of her ears and flicked his finger against the huge ruby surrounded by diamonds dangling from her earlobe. 'Was this jewellery, and the shiny bauble on your finger, your price for agreeing to marry my father?'

'I don't have a price.'

He gave a disbelieving snort. 'Tell me, Isla, why would a beautiful young woman choose to become engaged to an elderly billionaire if not for financial gain?'

Her temper flared at his implication that she was a fortune hunter. 'Do you think I'm a gold-digger?'

'Well done. I said you were clever,' he mocked.

The condemnation in Andreas's eyes was unjust. For a moment Isla was tempted to defend herself by explaining the truth about her relationship with his father. But she'd given her word to Stelios that she would keep his secret. A secret which was going to have huge implications for his family and possibly for his oil refining business. As yet Andreas was unaware that Karelis Corp was threatened by a hostile takeover bid from another company. Soon he would learn that her engagement to his father was intended to make Stelios appear strong and in control of the company, and Andreas might even thank her.

'Your father and I have an understanding…'

He swore, his voice low but no less savage. 'Does Stelios know about us?'

'Us?' Isla's brows lifted and she injected cool disdain into her tone. 'There has never been *us*.'

'We shared a scorching kiss at my father's house in London. *Theos!* The chemistry between us was explosive,' Andreas reminded her.

Heat spread across Isla's face. She needed no reminding of her uncharacteristically wanton behaviour. She had declined Stelios's invitation to join him and Andreas when she'd served coffee in the drawing room. Making the excuse that she was doing some baking, she had carefully not met Andreas's speculative gaze. But later he had returned the tea tray to the kitchen.

'Thanks. You can leave the cups in the sink,' she told him in a dismissive voice, hoping he would take the hint and return to his father. Her heart-rate quickened when he lounged against the kitchen counter.

'So you weren't lying,' he murmured, watching her take a tray of madeleines out of the oven. 'I assumed you'd said you were busy in the kitchen because you wanted to avoid me.'

'I never tell lies,' she said crisply, focusing her attention on lifting the delicate little cakes onto a cooling rack rather than look at Andreas. But she was fiercely aware of him, casually dressed in jeans that hugged his lean hips and a black T-shirt moulded to his muscular torso. His rampant masculinity disturbed her and the sensual musk of his aftershave in the warm kitchen assailed her senses.

'I'm glad to hear it. Perhaps you can explain why my father has fallen asleep in his armchair in the middle of the day. I know he is not getting any younger, but he has always had the energy of a man half his age.'

Weeks of gruelling chemotherapy had drained Stelios's strength, but Isla couldn't reveal to Andreas that his father was undergoing treatment for cancer. So much for her boast that she did not tell lies, she thought ruefully. 'Your father has been working hard recently,' she murmured. 'Why on earth would I want to avoid you?'

She had asked the question to distract attention away from Stelios's health—and her ploy worked. Andreas moved closer and there was a wicked gleam in his eyes as he slid his hand beneath her chin and tilted her face up to his.

'You tell me, *omorfia mou*. Do you think I haven't noticed the hungry looks you send me every time I pay my father a visit?'

'I don't...' she began, her face flaming with embarrassment that Andreas had guessed her fascination with him. It was so unlike her. She was always guarded with men, determined to protect her heart against the pain of rejection that she'd felt so deeply in the past. Andreas's sexy laugh sent a tremor through her and, fool that she was, Isla ignored her common sense which told her to step away from him.

'Yes, you do,' he drawled. 'What's more, you want me to kiss you.'

Her heart leapt into her throat. 'I do not...' she whispered, but her denial died away as he lowered his head until his lips were centimetres above hers and his warm breath grazed her skin.

'Liar.'

He had kissed her then. Although kiss was not an apt description of the way he had claimed her mouth with an arrogant possession that should have appalled her. Instead she had capitulated to his mastery, unable to resist his fiery passion and the bold sweep of his tongue between her lips.

The kiss was unlike anything Isla had ever experienced before. She had been kissed by other men—a few, although she could count on one hand the number of dates she'd been on that had got as far as a fumbling kiss at the end of the evening, she thought ruefully. When Andreas kissed her, she discovered a deeply sensual side to her nature that shocked her. But, before she had a chance to explore how he made her feel, he snatched his mouth from hers and stepped away from her so abruptly that she grabbed hold of the kitchen counter to support her legs that had turned to jelly. Andreas's hard-boned face gave no clue to his thoughts and he walked out of the kitchen without a word.

Isla felt humiliated by his rejection, which brought

back painful memories of when she'd been a teenager and had introduced herself to her father. With hindsight, perhaps she had been naïve to hope that David Stanford would be delighted to meet the daughter he'd abandoned when she was a few months old. But his insistence that there was no place for her in his life had been a brutal end to her hopes of having a relationship with her father. Isla had vowed then never to allow herself to be hurt by any man ever again.

She was jolted back to the present when she felt the pressure of Andreas's hard thigh against hers. She hadn't been aware that he'd moved, but now she found herself trapped against the balustrade. Her breath hitched in her throat when he ran his finger lightly down her hot cheek. She realised that she had been staring at his sensual mouth while she'd relived the kiss they had shared in London. The gleam in his eyes told her he had read her thoughts.

'Tell me about your romance with my father,' he demanded in a cynical voice. 'It seems very sudden. A few weeks ago you were employed as his housekeeper and you were quite happy to kiss me.'

'The kiss was a mistake that I immediately regretted.' She flushed at his look of arrogant disbelief. 'It's true. You're a playboy who uses women for your pleasure and discards them like trash when you are bored of them. You asked why I accepted your father's proposal and I'll tell you. Stelios is a gentleman. He is kind and sweet...'

Isla's voice thickened with emotion. Stelios was the only person, apart from her mother, who had ever cared about her, but soon he would be gone from this world, just as her mother had gone, and she would be alone again. The one tiny comfort was that Stelios and Marion would finally be together.

'You expect me to believe that my father's wealth has no bearing on your decision to accept his marriage proposal?' Andreas gritted.

'I don't care what you believe. The truth is that I love your father.'

Andreas jerked as if she'd slapped him. His blue eyes burned into Isla like lasers, seeking out every last secret in her soul as his dark head came closer, blotting out the light from the room behind him so that there was just the darkness of the night and the harsh sound of his breaths echoing the erratic beat of her heart.

'Love?' he mocked. He captured her wrist between his strong fingers. 'I could kiss you right now and you wouldn't stop me, even though my father, who you profess to love, and the guests he invited to celebrate his engagement to you are only feet away from us.'

He dropped his gaze to the exposed upper slopes of her breasts that were rising and falling jerkily. Isla knew she should demand that he release her. But she couldn't speak, could barely think. The spicy scent of his aftershave, mixed with something elusive and *male,* swamped her senses. His mouth, so close to hers but not close enough, was an unbearable torment. Heat swept through her and she felt an ache low in her pelvis. Her breasts felt heavy and she wanted… Oh, God, she wanted his mouth everywhere on her body.

Her tongue darted out to moisten her lips and Andreas swore. 'This is crazy,' he said hoarsely. He sounded as if he was waging an internal battle with himself and his voice jolted Isla to her senses.

She must be out of her mind to allow Andreas to undermine her defences. Even if she hadn't agreed to the pretend engagement with Stelios, it would be foolish to succumb to her desire for Andreas, which made her feel hot and shivery at the same time.

No other man had ever excited her the way Andreas did, and she longed to press herself against his whipcord body and burn in his fire. But the kiss they had shared in London had clearly meant nothing to him, she reminded herself, still smarting from the memory of how he had walked away from her without a backward glance. She would not be Andreas's plaything and she put her hand on his chest to push him away, not sure whether to be relieved or disappointed when he dropped his arms to his sides and stepped away from her.

Light spilled across the terrace from the drawing room as the door swung open and Stelios's slightly stooped figure was silhouetted in the doorframe. 'Isla?'

'I'm here,' she called out. She was still looking at Andreas and flushed at the contemptuous expression in his eyes when he stared back at her. Thank goodness she had come to her senses and stopped him from kissing her.

'What are you doing out here in the dark?' Stelios asked.

'I was pointing out the lights of some of the notable buildings on the mainland to Isla,' Andreas told his father, falling into step beside her when she walked back across the terrace. 'I explained that the villa stands on a hill, hence the excellent view.'

Stelios was silent as his eyes moved between Isla and his son. 'Yes, I see,' he said softly at last. Isla prayed he didn't. It was ridiculous to feel guilty, she told herself. Stelios had promised that he would explain to his family the reason for their fake engagement after Nefeli's birthday party. But the affection she felt for the elderly man was genuine and she smiled at him as she slipped her arm through his.

'I'm sorry you were looking for me. I should have told you that I was stepping outside for some fresh air.'

'Your advice is needed,' Stelios told her. 'My friend Georgios is planning to visit the British Museum in London and he is especially interested in seeing the collection of ancient Greek antiquities housed there. I explained that you will be able to advise him which galleries and exhibits he would enjoy.'

'Do you spend a lot of time in a museum, Isla?' Andreas's tone was sceptical.

'I work as an assistant curator in the Greek and Roman department at the British Museum. The position is part-time, allowing me to fit the hours around my job as your father's housekeeper in London, as well as studying for my PhD in classical civilisations.'

That wiped the smirk off Andreas's face, Isla thought with satisfaction as she allowed Stelios to escort her back into the salon to join the other guests. Andreas had accused her of being a gold-digger and she'd enjoyed his obvious surprise that she had a career. But she was annoyed with herself for caring about his opinion of her. Common sense told her that he was the last man on the planet she should be drawn to.

She glanced over her shoulder and saw that he had followed them into the salon and taken a drink from the butler. Andreas must have sensed her eyes on him and he turned his head to look directly at her, lifting his glass in mocking salute before he drained the amber liquid in one gulp. Isla watched the movement of his Adam's apple as he swallowed.

He was unashamedly masculine and she remembered how his body had felt as hard as steel when he'd trapped her up against the balustrade on the terrace with a muscular thigh. His olive-toned skin gleamed like bronze in the brightly lit room, and when he raked his hand carelessly through his dark hair her fingers itched to do the same.

Isla had never been this fascinated by a member of the opposite sex before. She had dated a few guys at university but was wary of being hurt and she'd never felt a desire for any of those relationships to progress as far as the bedroom, which was why she couldn't understand her response to Andreas. She did not like him and certainly didn't trust him, so why did he make her senses sing and bring her body to urgent life?

She had the unenviable title of the world's oldest virgin, Isla thought wryly. Although she doubted that Andreas would believe it. His cynical expression when he'd seen the sparkling diamond ring on her finger indicated that he was convinced she had used her feminine wiles to captivate his billionaire father.

CHAPTER THREE

ANDREAS'S FEET POUNDED on the sand where the waves rippled against the shore. The sun was climbing high in the sky and the temperature was already soaring. Usually he went for a run at the break of dawn when the day was fresh and full of possibilities. But he had woken late after a restless night. Sleep had eluded him for hours as he'd struggled to understand his behaviour the previous evening when he'd followed Isla out onto the terrace and been tempted to kiss her.

Theos, she had made him shake like a teenager at the mercy of his hormones. The chemistry between them had been almost tangible and if she hadn't pushed him away he doubted he would have been able to resist her. But the realisation that he could have been caught in a compromising situation with his father's fiancée had filled him with self-loathing. Even more incomprehensible was the fact that Isla had threatened his self-control with her mix of sensuality and innocence, which *couldn't* be real, he told himself.

He was convinced that Isla was a gold-digger. Andreas had learned from bitter personal experience that some women had no scruples and would do anything to get their hands on the Karelis fortune. His mouth thinned as he remembered the lies that an ex-girlfriend, Sadie, had told the media about him after he'd seen through her attempt to deceive him. He should have realised sooner that Sadie had been more interested in his bank balance than him. He would bet his entire fortune that Isla was attracted to his elderly father's wealth. Her air of vulnerability, which evoked a protective instinct in Andreas he hadn't known he possessed, was no doubt part of her clever act, he thought grimly.

He ran faster, pushing himself until his lungs burned. But when he reached the end of the bay—after passing the old fisherman's cottage that he'd turned into his private bolthole—and climbed the headland of volcanic rock, he barely noticed the stunning view of the crystalline turquoise sea. Instead he visualised Isla in her sexy red dress and remembered how soft her body had felt against his when she'd brushed past him on the terrace.

She had insisted that she loved Stelios. Of course she was bound to say that, Andreas brooded. But, for all his cynicism, he could not deny that there had been genuine emotion in her voice. Another thing which had thrown him was learning that she was highly educated and worked in a goddamn museum. If she had been an airhead it would be easier to dismiss her relationship with his father. Isla Stanford was an enigma. Andreas did not know what to make of her and it irritated the hell out of him.

On his way back to the villa his phone rang. 'You are sure about this?' he questioned the security officer who he'd asked to look into Isla's background. 'I see. That's very interesting. Keep digging, Theo.'

His father and Isla were sitting at the breakfast table on the terrace which overlooked the infinity pool. Andreas hoped to slip unnoticed into the house, but Stelios waved to him and with a faint sigh he walked towards the table.

'*Kalimera*, Papa, Isla,' he murmured in greeting. The thought briefly crossed his mind that his father looked thinner than when he'd seen him in London a month ago. But his gaze was drawn to Isla and he forgot everything else.

In contrast to the sex-bomb image she'd projected last night, this morning she looked as pure as the driven snow in a pale lemon sundress with narrow straps that revealed her delicate shoulders. It was the first time Andreas had seen her hair loose and he wished he could run his fingers through the mass of honey-gold silk that tumbled in soft waves down her back.

Frustration darkened his mood. His fascination with Isla was something he'd never experienced before. Women came and went in his life without making any impact on him. He enjoyed their company as long as it was on his terms and he liked sex uncomplicated by commitment. Perhaps he wanted Isla so badly because she was off limits, he derided himself. For a man who had discovered while he was still a teenager that he could have any woman he wanted with the minimum of effort on his part, the fact that she was unobtainable made her exciting.

But maybe the reason why his heart jolted against his ribs when he met her cool grey gaze was simply that Isla was breathtakingly lovely. Tearing his gaze from her, Andreas glanced at the pile of newspapers on the table. Most of the European tabloids carried a photo on the front page of Stelios looking into the eyes of his new fiancée while he pressed his lips against the enormous diamond on her finger.

Andreas had woken to the storm on social media created by his father's marriage plans. The announcement had resulted in a spike in Karclis Corp's share price on the stock market. Investors liked strong company leaders, and presumably the news that Stelios was planning to marry a woman decades younger than him proved that the old man was still a force to be reckoned with, Andreas thought sardonically.

'I am surprised that you decided to make a public statement about your engagement, Papa. You have previously been critical whenever my name has made the headlines.'

Stelios's lips thinned. 'A kiss-and-tell story by one of your disgruntled ex-lovers in a downmarket rag is not the same thing as an announcement about my future plans to the media.'

Andreas was genuinely curious. 'You have always kept your personal life separate from business but I understand that you invited journalists into the boardroom of Karelis Corp to make your announcement. I am merely pointing out that it is not like you to court the paparazzi.'

Was it his imagination or did Stelios seem relieved when the conversation was curtailed by the arrival of the butler bearing a jug of coffee? Moments later, Dinos's wife Toula, who had worked as the family's cook at the villa for as long as Andreas could remember, bustled across the terrace carrying a plate with his favourite breakfast of spinach and feta wrapped in filo pastry. He was fond of the couple, who had taken care of him when he was a boy and had been sent to stay on Louloudi in the school holidays because his mother had preferred him to be out of the way.

'I am happy that you no longer race your big motorbike,' Toula told him after they had exchanged greetings. She glanced heavenwards. 'Always I used to pray that you would be safe. When you had your accident I was so worried about you.'

'As you can see, I am fully recovered,' Andreas reassured her, automatically rubbing his hand over the long scar on his chest that was hidden beneath his running vest. The loss of his racing career was still painful and the scar was an ugly reminder of the accident during a race two years ago in which he'd suffered a ruptured aorta that had almost proved fatal.

'We are all glad that Andreas has finally seen sense and given up fooling around on motorbikes and riding them at ridiculous speeds,' Stelios said in a gruff tone.

Andreas's mouth tightened. He hadn't expected sympathy from his father, who had disapproved of his racing career. But the lecture he'd received while he had been recovering from his injuries had driven a wedge further between him and Stelios. It had been the same old rhetoric: Karelis Corp was his destiny and his duty.

'I was the Superbike World Champion for four consecutive years,' he reminded his father. 'The racing team which I own and manage is regarded as a world leader in the development of analytics used to modernise engine configuration testing, and Aeolus Racing has sponsorship worth millions of dollars. I would not call that *fooling around.*'

Stelios frowned. 'Your place is here in Greece, not in California. You know that I would like to retire and you should be preparing to take my place as head of the company.'

'You have spent much of your time in England for the past eighteen months,' Andreas pointed out. 'Every time I visited you in London I tried to talk about Karelis Corp, and in particular some worrying rumours I have heard about the company, but you refused to discuss things with me.'

A dark flush appeared on Stelios's face. 'I need to be sure of your commitment to Karelis Corp. If you spent less time womanising, and there were fewer stories about your personal life in the gutter press I would feel more confident about handing the most powerful role in the company over to you.'

Andreas gritted his teeth. 'You know full well that the woman who sold her story to the papers was lying.'

But the damage to his reputation had been done, Andreas thought bitterly. When lingerie model Sadie Barnes had told him she was pregnant with his child he'd asked for a paternity test. She had tearfully accused him of not trusting her, but he'd insisted on a test. Instead, Sadie had sold a story to the tabloids saying that Andreas had abandoned her and his unborn baby.

The media storm had broken on the day he was due to compete in a motorbike race which, had he won, would have given him the title of World Superbike Champion for a record fifth time. But an hour before the race Stelios had phoned Andreas and accused him of bringing shame to the name Karelis and damaging the company. The furious exchange of words with his father had, Andreas was sure, contributed to his lapse of concentration that had resulted in the high-speed crash.

'I accept that that particular story turned out to be untrue, but your playboy image is not good for Karelis Corp,' Stelios muttered. 'You should be thinking about marrying a suitable wife and settling down.' Andreas gave a snort of derision and Stelios rose to his feet and shook his head when Isla immediately stood up. 'Sit down and finish your breakfast, my dear.' He spoke to her in a softer voice than he had used to his son. 'I need to phone my lawyer and I'll go to my study to make the call.'

Isla looked as though she wanted to argue as she watched Stelios walk slowly towards the house. After a few moments she sat back down and glared at Andreas. Clearly she blamed him for the argument with Stelios. The truth was that he and his father were both strong-willed, but Stelios wanted an heir he could mould into his likeness, not a maverick son who was determined to make his own mark on the world.

Andreas scowled at the plate of food in front of him, his appetite suddenly non-existent. He felt taut and strung out and his mood turned blacker with the realisation that for once he had no control over his feelings. For the first time in his life he wished he was far away from Louloudi, far away from the woman who had such an unsettling effect on him.

The floral fragrance of Isla's perfume assailed him and his skin felt too tight for his body. He wondered what she would do if he walked around the table, leaned over and claimed her mouth with his. Would she respond to him as she had done in London? She had wanted him to kiss her on the terrace last night. Her eyes had flashed silver-bright with desire and he'd sensed the effort it had taken her to resist the attraction that blazed between them. He forced his mind back to the present when Isla spoke.

'Your father loves you, you know,' she said softly. 'He told me that he wishes the two of you were closer.'

Andreas was outraged that Stelios had discussed him with Isla. It felt like a betrayal. 'With respect,' he said grittily, 'my relationship with my father is none of your damn business.'

'I was simply trying to help. I care about Stelios…'

He snorted. 'You sound convincing, but unlike my father I am not the least bit taken in by the role of ingénue that you play so well. Let's face it, Stelios is not the first wealthy old man to be susceptible to your charms. A few years ago you inherited a substantial sum of money from a Major Charles Walters who you had befriended.'

'It's true that I was friends with Charles and his wife Enid. I was shocked when I learned that they had left me a bequest but there was nothing grubby or underhand about it.' Hectic colour flared on Isla's cheeks. 'They were an elderly, childless couple who owned the manor house in the village where I grew up, and they were patrons of the local school. When I was a teenager I had a part-time cleaning job at the manor, and Charles and Enid encouraged my hope of going to university. They died within a few months of each other and left legacies to several young people in the village with the stipulation that the money was to go towards paying university fees. Without their generosity, I would have graduated with a huge debt and struggled to continue with my studies.' She frowned. 'How did you know I had been left some money?'

'You were investigated,' he told her smoothly, watching her grey eyes flash with anger. It gave him a sense of satisfaction knowing he'd rattled her. 'My family are one of the wealthiest in Greece and, although security here on Louloudi is discreet, I asked the protection team to run some checks on you. My father especially is at risk of being kidnapped and held to ransom by criminal gangs.'

'I'm not a *criminal*.' Isla's finely arched brows drew together in a frown. 'Does Stelios know that you had me investigated?'

'Does he know that you inherited money from another wealthy old man?' Andreas countered to avoid answering her question.

'Your father knows everything about me.'

She met Andreas's gaze across the table and he found himself looking away first, shaken by the honesty in her expression. There was something else, an inexplicable sadness. The shimmer of tears made her grey eyes glisten like wet slate. She was a damn good actress, he thought grimly, but he refused to fall for her little-girl-lost look.

Isla stood up and Andreas was aware of the hard thud of his pulse as the breeze flattened her dress against her body, revealing the swell of her breasts and the gentle curve of her hips. 'I wish you would believe that I mean your father no harm.'

'Stelios doesn't seem to be himself.' Andreas also got to his feet, frowning as he remembered how exhausted his father had been at the end of the dinner party.

Isla hesitated. 'He has been working hard.'

The gentle affection in her voice for Stelios evoked a feeling in Andreas that he refused to acknowledge was envy. His mother had not shown him tenderness or affection when he was a child, and since he'd reached adulthood he'd avoided emotional relationships, assuring himself that he neither wanted nor needed love. He swore silently, irritated that Isla made him question the status quo of his life that he'd been perfectly content with until now.

'Perhaps Stelios is tired for another reason,' he growled. Isla looked puzzled and he elaborated. 'You are a lot younger than my father and he might be wearing himself out trying to keep you happy in the bedroom.'

'Your father and I are not lovers,' she said stiffly.

'Why not?' Andreas's eyes narrowed when she did not answer. 'I'm curious about your relationship with Stelios. I watched the two of you at dinner last night and I'd swear you do not feel any sexual attraction for my father.'

'Not everything is about sex,' she snapped. 'Relationships—meaningful relationships, not the love-'em-and-leave-'em kind that you only seem capable of—are about mutual respect, friendship and trust.'

Andreas frowned, unsettled by her fervent words. In an ideal relationship those were the qualities he would want. But he did not believe in happy ever after. Isla certainly sounded convincing, but he was sure she had an ulterior motive for wanting to marry his father. His conscience pricked that he *wanted* to believe the worst of her. If he believed that she was untrustworthy, it might end his annoying fascination with her. His jaw hardened.

'My guess is that you are determined to make Stelios wait until after he has married you before you will allow him to take you to bed. As his wife you will have access to his fortune.'

Isla drew an audible breath and swung her hand up to his face, but Andreas's reactions were quicker and he captured her wrist before she could strike him. 'I wouldn't,' he advised softly.

'You have a vile mind.' She was breathing hard and her breasts rose and fell jerkily. Her grey eyes darkened with temper but Andreas could feel the pulse in her wrist beating erratically beneath his thumb. The air between them prickled with sexual awareness and he was certain that Isla felt it as intensely as he did. Her voice cracked when she spoke. 'I'm not surprised that Stelios doesn't—' She broke off and dropped her gaze from his.

'My father doesn't approve of me. Is that what you were going to say?' he drawled. It shouldn't hurt as much as it did. He and Stelios hadn't seen eye to eye for years.

'He doesn't feel able to confide in you,' Isla muttered. 'I wish you would talk to Stelios and resolve the differences between you, before...'

'Before…what?' Andreas's brows rose. But whatever Isla had been about to say she clearly thought better of it. She pulled her wrist out of his grasp and turned and walked away. He watched her go and cursed beneath his breath.

The differences between him and his father were not easily resolvable. Stelios had been a largely absent parent when Andreas was young, spending the majority of his time running Karelis Corp, and later with his English mistress. But Andreas was no longer a teenager who saw everything as black or white. He understood how his mother's poor health—she'd often reminded him that she had suffered a stroke due to complications during his birth—must have put a strain on his parents' relationship. He had never felt loved by either of them. He was the Karelis heir, born and raised to take over the company which had been started by his great-grandfather. His father had not forgiven him for putting his motorbike racing career ahead of his duty—especially as Stelios had put duty to his family before his personal happiness.

Nefeli's birthday party could not come round soon enough, Andreas brooded as he resumed his seat at the table and forced himself to eat the *spanakopita* that Toula had made for him. In a few days he would return to California and concentrate on managing Aeolus Racing. Maybe he'd look up the redhead who had flirted with him in a bar before he'd left for Greece. It was weeks since he'd had sex, and celibacy was not a natural state for him. Frustration was no doubt the reason for his inconvenient attraction to his father's fiancée.

CHAPTER FOUR

FROM HER BEDROOM window in the villa Isla could see a dozen luxury tents which had been erected on the lawn in the garden below. They would provide sleeping accommodation for Nefeli's many friends who would be staying on Louloudi for the weekend. It was glamping rather than camping, Isla thought wryly, remembering the few holidays that she and her mum had spent in a tent in very wet Wales. Not that the weather or a tight budget had spoiled their fun. Marion had made everything an adventure, and they had been so close. Her mum had been her best friend and Isla still missed her. Swallowing hard, she forced her thoughts away from the past.

Every bedroom in the villa was occupied by members of the extended Karelis family. For the past two days extensive preparations had been underway for Nefeli's twenty-first birthday party and an air of general chaos pervaded the house. No expense had been spared, and Isla had been amazed by the number of crates of champagne unloaded from the boat which had also brought an army of caterers and other staff to the island.

Stelios was determined that his daughter's birthday party would be perfect. But when Isla knocked on the door of his private suite before she walked in, she found him slumped in an armchair with his eyes closed. The past few days had taken their toll on his strength but he was adamant that no one must know about his illness until he was ready to break the news to his family.

'Is that the dress you are planning to wear tonight?'

'I thought you were asleep.' She smiled at the man who had come to mean so much to her. Stelios was like the father she'd never had. 'Yes.' She ran her hand down the skirt of her oyster-coloured evening gown. The dress had a high neck and long sleeves. Memories of the attraction that had flared between her and Andreas when she'd worn the low-cut red dress two nights ago had been behind her decision to cover up.

She had hardly seen him since he had accused her of being a gold-digger, and she sensed that for the past few days he had deliberately avoided her. But the previous day she had gone to the pool and slipped off her robe in preparation to climb down the steps into the water. She'd hesitated when she'd heard a familiar sexy voice say her name, and silently cursed herself for not noticing that Andreas was down at the other end of the pool.

He swam up to the shallow end with powerful strokes. When he stood up, she noticed a long red scar on his chest that sliced all the way down his abdomen.

Water droplets glistened in the whorls of dark hairs that covered his chest and arrowed over his flat stomach. Of their own accord Isla's eyes lowered to his black swim shorts that sat low on his hips, and her mouth went dry.

'Come on in. The pool is heated—and you look cold,' he drawled.

'I'm not cold.' Following his gaze, she looked down and was mortified to see the hard points of her nipples jutting beneath her bikini top. The air around the pool suddenly felt stiflingly hot, and her awareness of Andreas was so intense that Isla's skin prickled. 'Actually, I've changed my mind about having a swim,' she muttered, quickly pulling her robe back on.

'Coward,' he called after her mockingly as she hurried away.

'Isla?' Stelios's voice jolted Isla back to the present, and she hoped he would not query why her face that she could see reflected in the mirror was suffused with colour. 'You look charming, my dear,' Stelios told her. 'But it will be better if you wear a more eye-catching outfit.'

'I don't want to look as though I am in competition with Nefeli at her party,' Isla murmured. The young Greek girl's unfriendly attitude had made it clear how much Nefeli resented her presence on Louloudi.

Stelios closed his eyes once more and Isla bit her lip as she studied him. His skin was grey and his cheekbones were prominent where he had lost weight, but he was desperate to hide the signs of his illness from his family for a little longer.

She sighed. 'I'll choose a different dress.'

'Wear the blue Oscar de la Renta.'

Ten minutes later, Isla returned to Stelios's suite wearing the dress he had suggested. 'You wanted eye-catching and this certainly fits the bill,' she said ruefully. The midnight blue dress was blatantly sexy with a plunging neckline and off-the-shoulder straps. It was made from satin overlaid with chiffon which had a sparkle of silver thread running through the material so that the dress shimmered. The side split in the skirt revealed her leg all the way up to her thigh when she walked. Silver high-heeled shoes gave her an extra four inches of height.

'No one will take any notice of me, and all eyes will be on you,' Stelios said with satisfaction. He handed her a velvet box and Isla gasped as she lifted out a diamond choker.

'I'm only borrowing it for tonight,' she insisted as she fastened the exquisite piece of jewellery around her neck.

'I need you to sparkle this evening,' Stelios told her. 'Nefeli and Andreas must not guess that the party is the last event I will be here to celebrate with them.'

'You don't know that,' Isla whispered. 'The specialist said you could have months left.'

Stelios levered himself slowly out of the armchair. 'You remind me of your mother in so many ways. Not only in your looks. You have Marion's gentleness and compassion. I am so glad that I met you again, Isla. The last time you were just a little girl and now you are a beautiful young woman. One day I hope you will fall in love with a man who will treasure you.'

Fat chance, Isla thought to herself as she followed Stelios out of his suite and they descended the marble staircase. Love was a fool's game, and she must be the biggest fool of all because she could not control the frantic thud of her heart when she walked into the ballroom and the first person she saw—the only person she saw in the crowded room—was Andreas.

He wore 'formal' with the easy air of a man who had been born into wealth and privilege. The Karelis heir in all his spectacularly handsome glory. His tuxedo drew the eye to his broad shoulders and narrow black trousers emphasised his lean, athletic build. Beneath the fine white silk of his shirt, Isla saw the shadow of his black chest hairs. His sophisticated clothes could not hide his raw masculinity and she felt an ache in her womb, a longing for something she could not explain to herself.

The woman hanging onto his arm was exotically beautiful. She had long dark hair cascading over one shoulder and looked as though she had been poured into her sequined green dress. Isla refused to acknowledge a stab of jealousy as she watched Andreas dip his head towards his companion and murmur something in her ear. The intimacy between them suggested that they were lovers. Not that she cared in the slightest who Andreas slept with, she told herself firmly.

Perhaps he sensed her scrutiny for he looked in her direction. Heat blazed in his eyes as he skimmed them over her, moving from her hair, piled in an elaborate chignon on top of her head, down to the daring neckline of her dress and lower to her bared thigh, exposed by the split in the skirt. Finally his gaze rested on the diamond choker around her neck and his lips twisted in a sardonic expression, before he turned his attention back to his glamorous companion.

Isla felt a hollow sensation in her stomach. Why was she allowing a notorious playboy like Andreas to get to her? she wondered. She had promised herself when she was sixteen and her father had dismissed her as if she was a nonentity that she would never again put herself in a position where a man made her feel vulnerable.

Resolutely, she pinned a smile on her lips and slipped her hand through Stelios's arm so that he could lean on her without it being obvious to the other guests. She had a role to play, Isla reminded herself. Stelios wanted her to sparkle and distract attention away from him, and she set about doing just that.

Much later in the evening when she noticed the lines of strain on Stelios's face, Isla ignored his protest and steered him across the ballroom to a sofa in a quiet corner of the room. 'Rest for a while,' she urged, her heart contracting when he gave a low groan of relief as he sank down onto the cushions. 'The party is a great success and Nefeli looks like she is having a wonderful time.'

She moved her eyes from Stelios's daughter, who was dancing with a group of her friends, and felt a stab of pain when she saw Andreas wrapped around a lissom brunette wearing a figure-hugging silver dress. 'Andreas also seems to be enjoying himself,' she said flatly as she became aware that Stelios had followed her gaze.

'I have a feeling that you disapprove of my son,' he murmured. 'Why is that?'

'I… I hardly know him.' Isla felt her cheeks grow warm. She was flustered by Stelios's question, afraid that she had unwittingly revealed her fascination with Andreas. 'I'm sure he's very nice,' she said lamely.

Stelios chuckled. 'I have never heard Andreas described as "nice" before.' He gave her an odd look. 'My son is a complicated man, but his heart is in the right place.'

'Can I get you another drink, or some canapés?' Isla said quickly, keen to move the conversation away from Andreas's heart, which she seriously doubted existed.

Stelios shook his head. 'I'll just sit here. I am feeling a little breathless. But you should go and dance.'

'I'd rather keep you company.' She had stayed at his side all evening and chatted to the other guests. Most people spoke at least a little English, and she had learned to speak modern Greek at the same time as she had been studying ancient Greek history. But Isla was not a natural social butterfly and she felt uncomfortable being the centre of attention. She was surprised that no one had commented on how frail Stelios looked, but he had been a powerful figure for so long and she guessed that he was seen as invincible by his family and business associates.

Her eyes moved back to the dance floor and she saw that Nefeli was dancing with Andreas. Isla's heart missed a beat when the tune finished and brother and sister walked over to where she and Stelios were sitting.

'Papa, will you come and dance with me?' Nefeli ignored Isla and held out her hand imperiously to her father.

'Why don't you take my place?' Isla said quickly, standing up and indicating the empty space she had vacated on the sofa. 'Your father was just saying that he would like to spend some time with you on your birthday.' There was no harm in a white lie if it meant that Stelios could remain sitting, she told herself.

'An excellent idea,' Andreas murmured. 'We'll leave these two alone while you dance with me, Isla.'

The gleam in his eyes sent her heart slamming against her ribcage but she couldn't think of an excuse to refuse him. Determined that he would not guess the effect he had on her, she held herself stiffly when he placed his hand between her shoulder blades and propelled her towards the dance floor. To make matters worse, the DJ changed the tempo of the music from disco to a slow number that prompted the couples around them to move into each other's arms.

'Relax, I don't bite,' Andreas said drily as he captured her hand in his and splayed the fingers of his other hand over her naked back, drawing her closer so that her body brushed against his. The split in her skirt had fallen open and she could feel his hard thigh muscle against her stocking-clad thigh. 'You look incredible in that dress.' His warm breath tickled her ear. 'Are you enjoying the party?'

Isla could not tell him that she longed for the party to be over because she knew it was an ordeal for Stelios. And she was certainly not going to admit that watching Andreas dance with a constant stream of beautiful women had evoked a sensation like sharp knives stabbing her in her stomach. She shrugged. 'Yes, of course. Your father is pleased that it has gone well.'

'You really care about him, don't you?'

Her eyes flew to his face and she expected to see his usual cynical expression, but he was looking at her intently as if he was trying to read her thoughts. Isla hoped that he couldn't because her thoughts were decidedly X-rated.

Andreas danced with a natural grace and rhythm. He moved his hand down and rested it at the base of her spine, drawing her subtly closer so that they were hip to hip. She was shocked to feel the rigid evidence of his arousal and knew he felt the tremor that ran through her when he swore softly and clamped her hard against him. Even though she was wearing four-inch heels she was much shorter than him, and her gaze was focused on his jaw, shaded with black stubble, that she remembered had felt abrasive on her skin that time he'd kissed her in London.

'Of course I care about Stelios,' she said, forcing her mind away from the dangerous path it seemed intent on following.

'But you are not in love with my father and he is not in love with you.' Andreas tightened his hold around her waist when she attempted to pull herself out of his arms. She discovered that while they had been dancing he had steered them towards the door of the ballroom. Without giving her a chance to protest, he whisked her out to the entrance hall and across to the library.

'Well?' he demanded after he closed the library door and leaned his back against it, crossing his arms over his chest. 'What is the truth about your relationship with my father?'

'Why don't you ask him?' Isla prevaricated.

'I'm asking you.'

She stayed silent and Andreas shrugged. 'I'm prepared to stand here all night until you give me a believable answer. If you are not interested in Stelios's money, and I am convinced from my observations of the two of you that you do not have a physical relationship with my father, why did you agree to marry him?'

It would be wrong for her to betray Stelios's trust and reveal that he was dying. But Isla felt guilty that she could not be honest with Andreas. She chewed her bottom lip and then gave a heavy sigh. 'I met Stelios many years ago when I was a child.'

Andreas looked puzzled. 'Where did you meet him?'

'He was friendly with my mother. Mum worked for a company in England which had been bought by Karelis Corp. She was Stelios's secretary but their relationship developed and they became…close.' Her voice faltered when Andreas frowned. 'I was very young but I remember that Stelios used to come and stay with us.'

'Are you saying that your mother was my father's mistress?'

'You make it sound tawdry but Mum was in love with Stelios and he loved her,' Isla said defensively. 'I can only have been four or five, but I remember it was a happy time. My mum even asked me if I would like Stelios to be my father.'

Andreas swore. 'He was already a father to me and my sister. Nefeli was a baby when he went off to play happy families with you and your mother in England.'

She bit her lip. 'I was too young to have understood that Stelios had a family in Greece.'

'Your mother must have been aware that Stelios was being unfaithful to his wife. Where was your father?'

'I have no idea. He left when I was a few months old.'

'So your mother became a rich man's mistress.'

Isla's grey eyes flashed. 'Mum loved your father. She never met anyone else after he stopped coming to visit. She didn't talk about him, and I had more or less forgotten him, but when she died I found letters that

Stelios had written to her. In one letter he explained that he couldn't bear to be separated from his son and daughter and had decided to remain in Greece with his family. It was a tragic love story.'

She glared at Andreas when he gave a snort of derision. 'Stelios fell in love with my mother but there was no happy ending. After your mother died he came to England to look for Mum, but she had been killed six months earlier. I was struggling to cope with my grief. I had to move out of the house where we'd lived together because I couldn't afford to pay the rent on my income alone, and Stelios offered me a job as his housekeeper. He helped me when I was at my lowest, and when he was…' Just in time she stopped herself from revealing that Stelios had been diagnosed with cancer. 'Your father was lonely and he asked me to marry him.'

Andreas frowned. 'Why did you accept his proposal?'

She was digging herself deeper into a hole, Isla thought ruefully. 'Stelios is very charming and, as I said, he had been kind to me when I was a child. He promised to look after me.'

'So you regard him as a sort of father figure?'

'Something like that,' she mumbled.

Andreas's eyes narrowed. 'What about passion? You are a beautiful woman in the prime of your life and you must have a woman's needs.'

Isla felt herself blush. 'Sex isn't a big deal for me.'

'I don't believe that.' He uncrossed his arms and

walked towards her. The evocative scent of his after-shave sent a shiver of awareness through her. 'You say that sex is not important to you but your response to me suggests you are lying. Maybe it's simply that you haven't met a man who can unlock your desires?'

'And you think you are that man?' She tried to sound scornful but her voice was high-pitched and fraught with emotions she was desperate to hide.

'Perhaps,' Andreas murmured. 'Your body betrays you so beautifully.' He lifted his hand and placed his thumb pad over the pulse beating unevenly at the base of her throat.

Isla caught her breath when he lowered his gaze to the outline of her nipples that had hardened betrayingly beneath her dress. His blue eyes glittered. 'I know you want me. You will be making a mistake if you marry my father.'

She felt something sharp and intense coil inside her, a longing that she must deny. 'Do you find it so hard to accept that not every woman on the planet wants to sleep with you?'

His hands dropped to his sides. 'You can deny it as much as you like.' His voice was harsher, scraping across her skin so that she felt raw. 'But this is real and you feel it as much as I do.'

She did not need him to explain what he meant. *This* was the intangible alchemy that shimmered between them and threatened to burst into flame with a shared look. She had never felt anything like it before. Every cell in her body thrummed with awareness of Andreas, but her reaction to him terrified her.

She sensed that he could strip away everything she thought she knew about herself if she allowed him to get too close. But from now on she would be on her guard against him, Isla assured herself as she pushed past him and hurried out of the library.

CHAPTER FIVE

STELIOS WAS ASLEEP when Isla popped into his suite to check if he needed anything. She made sure that a glass of water and his tablets were within his reach on the bedside table. The evening had drained him but he had insisted on remaining at the party until after the fireworks display at midnight. Only then had she persuaded him to leave Nefeli and her friends to continue celebrating.

The young people's voices and laughter drifted up from the tents in the garden and Isla crossed the room and closed the window. Her gaze was drawn to the sea in the distance, dappled by the silver moonlight. It was almost one a.m. but she felt too restless to sleep. She hadn't seen Andreas again after she'd left him in the library and she'd felt annoyed with herself for scanning the ballroom for him. The truth was that he made her feel alive and without his presence the party had seemed flat.

She returned to stand by the bed, listening to Stelios's regular breathing. In the next day or so he would tell his family that he had terminal cancer, and the reason for their fake engagement would no longer be necessary, in private at least. But she had agreed to maintain the pretence of being his fiancée in public until after he'd announced that he was handing over the leadership of Karelis Corp to his son. It was important, Stelios had reiterated, that news of his illness was not made public and he continued to be seen as a powerful leader of the company. Once Andreas became CEO, Isla would be free to return to London and her job at the museum, leaving Stelios to spend his precious final weeks with his family.

Reassured that he was unlikely to stir for many hours, she left him and went to her own room. It was a relief to kick off her high heels and exchange her ball-gown for comfortable jersey shorts and a cotton strap top. She pulled the pins out of her chignon and shook her hair loose, and then slid her feet into leather flip-flops and stepped out into the corridor.

The staff had finished clearing away after the party and the house was quiet. She paused outside Andreas's door, wondering if he was asleep or if one of the gorgeous women who had flocked round him at the party was sharing his bed. Jerking her mind away from images of him and a lover naked and entwined in each other's arms, she went downstairs and out of the house.

Avoiding the garden, she followed a path that led directly to the beach, kicked off her flip-flops and walked across the soft sand. The night was warm and still, the air filled with the scent of the white sand lilies which grew in the dunes and a faint salt tang from the sea. Lost in her thoughts, Isla strolled along the shoreline until the lights from the garden were distant and the stars in the inky sky sparkled as brightly as the diamond choker she had returned to Stelios after the party.

He had tried to persuade her to keep the necklace and the other jewellery she'd worn in her role as his fiancée, but she'd refused. 'You will keep the ring though, won't you?' he'd said when she removed the huge diamond from her finger and placed it in the safe with the choker. 'You have helped me greatly and I want to give you something to remember me by.'

'I'll always remember you,' she had told him softly. Now tears blurred her vision as she stood on the beach, alone beneath the vast heavens.

'I know a cure for insomnia.' The familiar cynical voice came from behind her. Isla spun round and felt her heart collide painfully with her ribs when she made out Andreas sprawled on a slab of rock further up the beach. Behind him was the cottage she'd noticed when she'd walked this way along the beach once before. In the moonlight she saw that the front door was ajar.

Andreas sat upright and proffered the bottle he was holding. 'Bourbon is a cure for most ills, I find.'

'I don't drink spirits. In fact I rarely drink alcohol at all.' She bit her lip when she realised how strait-laced she sounded.

Andreas lifted the bottle to his lips and took a swig.

He had discarded his jacket and his bow tie hung loose around his neck. The top few buttons of his shirt were undone and his dark hair fell across his brow, adding to his rakishly sexy appearance. 'You should try it. Who knows, it might help you to loosen up a bit.'

'The man who killed my mother was found to be four times above the legal alcohol limit for driving.'

He swore softly. Isla turned her back on him and stared at the mysterious sea. She had no idea why she had told Andreas about her mum. The bereavement counsellor she'd seen a few times had suggested that talking about the accident might help her come to terms with the tragedy, but mostly she buried her feelings deep inside her and put on a brave face to the world.

'What happened?' Andreas's voice was suddenly close, and Isla gave a start when she discovered that he had moved silently and was standing beside her.

She shrugged. 'Mum was driving home from the call centre where she worked. She'd finished a late shift and the pubs had just closed. The other car hit her head-on. Miraculously, the driver escaped with minor injuries but Mum was killed instantly. In court the driver gave the excuse that he'd got drunk after breaking up with his girlfriend. The judge banned him from driving but didn't send him to prison because it was a first offence and it was felt that he deserved another chance. I wish Mum had been given a second chance.' She could not keep the bitterness out of her voice. 'She was forty-seven when she died.'

'I'm sorry.' The sympathy in Andreas's husky tone tugged on Isla's heart. She felt brittle, as if she might shatter. He moved to stand in front of her and slid his hand beneath her chin to tip her face up to his. She closed her eyes, not wanting him to see her emotions, which were still too raw. A tear slipped from beneath her lashes and she felt him gently brush it away with his thumb. 'When?'

'Two and a half years ago.'

'We have something in common. My mother died two years ago.'

'I know.' She opened her eyes and saw compassion in his gaze. The gleam of the moon made his face all angles and shadows. 'Stelios told me that your mother died a few weeks before you nearly lost your own life in a motorbike race. Were you close to her?'

It was odd how natural it felt when Andreas draped his arm across her shoulders and drew her towards him. Isla knew that she should pull away, and she would in a moment, she told herself. But her aching heart was comforted by this brief connection to another human being.

'No. I was sent away to boarding school at a young age. My grandmother was an American heiress who had married my Greek grandfather, and I spent most school holidays with my relatives in California or I was sent here to Louloudi.'

Andreas shrugged. 'I wasn't close to either of my parents. My father was busy running Karelis Corp and spent a lot of time away from home. When my mother discovered that he had a mistress in England, Stelios told her he wanted to end their marriage.'

Isla felt uncomfortable even though she knew there was no reason for her to feel guilty about her mum's relationship with Stelios. 'Was your mother upset when she found out about the affair?'

'My parents' marriage had been arranged. It was a business merger rather than a love match. Such things were not uncommon in Greek families years ago,' he added, catching Isla's shocked expression. 'They got on well enough until my mother learned of his infidelity and she was devastated.'

'You said that your parents hadn't been in love.'

'Stelios did not love my mother but she loved him.' Andreas exhaled heavily. 'My father wanted a divorce. I was a headstrong twelve-year-old and when I saw my mother crying I told Stelios that if he left the family I would never speak to him again. I forced him to choose between his English mistress and his heir.'

'He chose you,' Isla said quietly. 'Surely it shows that Stelios loved you?'

'He chose me because it was his duty to prepare me for power and leadership of Karelis Corp. But he resented me, especially when I was determined to pursue my own career and lead a different life to the one he had mapped out for me.'

Isla did not know what to say. She had been so young when Stelios had briefly been a father figure in her life, and of course she'd had no idea that he had a family in another country. It was a little less than two years ago, when Stelios had turned up at the house where she had lived with her mum and said that he was searching for Marion Christie, that Isla had learned the truth.

A low rumble of thunder pulled her from her thoughts. While she and Andreas had been talking a breeze had whipped up and raindrops the size of pennies stung her bare arms.

He captured her hand in his and pulled her up the beach. 'We'll shelter in the cottage.'

Within seconds the rain turned to a deluge and by the time they reached the cottage Isla was drenched. She followed Andreas through the front door. 'Wait here,' he ordered.

Moments later a flickering light filled the room as he lit a paraffin lamp and hung it on a hook on the wall. 'There's no electricity here,' he explained. 'The house is an original cottage from when the island was inhabited by a small community of fishermen and their families. The last family moved to the mainland many years ago and my grandfather bought Louloudi and commissioned the villa to be built. I renovated this place myself.'

Isla looked around the small sitting room, which had white-painted walls and bleached wooden ceiling beams. The room was simply furnished with a sofa and armchair covered with brightly coloured throws. A tiny kitchen led off the sitting room, and she thought how lovely it would be to prepare a meal on the rustic table with the sound of the waves breaking on the shore.

She imagined if she and Andreas were lovers relaxing over a leisurely breakfast after a night of passionate lovemaking. She hadn't lied when she'd told him that sex wasn't a big deal to her. She'd even wondered if she was frigid. But when she looked at his handsome face and imagined his sensual mouth claiming hers, the ache low in her pelvis became a throb of need that she had never experienced before.

It was as if she had been in a deep sleep until he had awoken her desire with his kiss. But Andreas was no Prince Charming, she reminded herself. Being trapped in the cottage with him was dangerous, but he was not the danger. It was the way he made her feel that both terrified and excited her.

She had prided herself on being cautious and sensible while the other girls she'd shared digs with at university had thrown themselves into love affairs that too often ended badly. Isla had allowed men to think she was unapproachable as a defence mechanism. The legacy of her father's rejection had made her a coward, she realised with sudden insight. She was twenty-five but she'd never been naked with a man, let alone had a physical relationship.

Telling Andreas about the accident that had claimed her mum's life, and seeing Stelios's health decline, were painful reminders that life was short and she had spent too long mired in hurts of the past. Andreas tempted her to lower her defensive barriers, especially when the fierce gleam in his eyes told her that he found her desirable.

'Storms are fairly common on the coast at this time of year but they tend to blow through quickly.' His voice pulled Isla from her thoughts and she watched him light a second paraffin lamp. He passed the lamp to her. 'Feel free to take a look around. There is a gas hob in the kitchen and I can make coffee if you would like some.'

'No, thanks.' Caffeine at this time of the night—it was actually morning, Isla amended—would not help her to fall asleep when she returned to the villa.

Holding the lamp aloft, she inspected the pretty blue-and-white-tiled kitchen and the shower room next door. A narrow hallway led to the only bedroom, and here the walls were unpainted, leaving the sand-coloured bricks exposed. The one big window had wooden shutters which were closed. In the centre of the room was a four-poster bed with white voile drapes. She stopped just inside the doorway, her gaze drawn to the bed. The sound of the rain drumming on the roof of the single-storey cottage made the bedroom, lit by the warm glow from the lamp, feel like a safe haven from the elements.

Footsteps on the stone floor behind her caused the tiny hairs of her body to stand on end. 'In daylight you must have a wonderful view from the bed,' she murmured.

'The view from where I'm standing right now is pretty good.' Andreas's deep voice rolled through her, and her heart missed a beat when she slowly turned around and found him close to her. She caught her breath when he dropped his gaze and stared at her vest top clinging damply to her breasts. Her nipples stood to attention and the husky groan he made caused Isla's stomach muscles to clench.

He took the lamp from her nerveless fingers and hung it on the wall. The sound of the storm raging outside became distant and she was aware of the unevenness of her breathing, *his*.

'I should go.' Common sense dictated that she should leave but her feet refused to move. She should have run back to the villa the moment she'd spotted Andreas on the beach, Isla thought ruefully. Instead she had walked towards him, forgetting her loyalty to Stelios, compelled by a force, a *need* that was beyond her control.

She had been surprised when Andreas revealed that his relationship with both his parents had been difficult. Isla sensed that his public image as a charismatic playboy hid a far more complex man— a man she wanted to know better. The truth was she was fascinated by him and she swallowed audibly when he lifted his hand and smoothed a few damp strands of her hair off her face.

'Stay until the storm has passed.' His voice was a low growl.

Isla wasn't sure if he meant the storm outside or the one that had simmered between them since they had been on the island. When he slowly lowered his head towards her she couldn't move, could hardly breathe. She wanted him to kiss her. There was no point pretending otherwise. She'd dreamed of his mouth on hers since he'd kissed her in London a month ago, and tonight, when her emotions were all over the place, he was something solid and safe to cling to in the storm—although the idea that this man represented safety would be laughable if she were able to think straight.

She felt the whisper of Andreas's warm breath on her cheek. He curled his hands over her shoulders, drawing her closer to his big, hard body. And then he brought his mouth down on hers and there was nothing but the intoxicating pleasure of his kiss. It was no gentle seduction but a ravishment of her senses as he increased the pressure of his lips and forced hers apart, allowing his tongue access to the moist heat of her mouth.

Isla sensed that Andreas had been fighting his attraction as much as she had, but tonight the barriers had come crashing down and their desire for each other was an unstoppable force. She succumbed utterly to his mastery, tipping her head back so that he could plunder her lips with a bone-shaking sensuality while she wrapped her arms around his neck and anchored herself to his strength.

He threaded one hand into her hair and ran his other hand down her body, cupping a breast and stroking his thumb over the nipple jutting beneath her damp top. The sensation was exquisite and a shudder ran through her as desire obliterated every sane thought and left only a greedy, aching need. She pressed herself closer to him when he shoved his hand under her top and spread his fingers possessively over her breast.

'Lift your arms up,' he said in a voice roughened by desire. The realisation that he was as powerless to resist the chemistry between them as she was dismissed the last of Isla's doubts. She lifted her arms and her heart thudded when he pulled the strap top over her head and then rocked back on his heels, his eyes glittering like blue flames as he stared at her bare breasts. 'You're so beautiful.' Dull colour winged along his high cheekbones. 'I sound like a bloody schoolboy.' He swore softly. *'Se thelo.'*

Isla knew the Greek words meant *I want you*. Desire hardened his features so that he looked feral with a hunger in his gaze that should have terrified her. But when he swept her up into his arms and carried her over to the bed she trembled, not with fear but a stark longing to feel his mouth on hers once again. To feel his mouth everywhere.

In a moment she would stop him, she assured herself. And she did not doubt that he would stop if she asked him to. Instinctively, she knew that Andreas would respect her wishes. But, like a drug addict desperate for her next fix, she was impatient for him to kiss her again. He laid her on the bed and she curled her arms around his neck, urging his mouth down onto hers.

Just one more kiss and then she would leave. Just one more. Her breath snagged in her throat when he trailed his lips down her neck and across the slope of one breast. He closed his mouth around her taut nipple and the effect of him sucking her felt like an explosion ripping through her, sensation building on sensation and sending a flood of heat right there between her legs where she ached so badly. Her body was unprepared for such an intensity of pleasure and when he captured her other nipple between his lean fingers and teased the turgid peak Isla lost all sense of who she was, of where she was.

Andreas had loosened the cord that held back the voile drapes and the filmy material surrounded the bed, separating them from the world outside, it seemed. Cocooning Isla from reality. Because this could not be real. She had fallen into a wonderful dream and she didn't want it to end. Her stomach muscles clenched involuntarily beneath the weight of his hand trailing over her abdomen and lower, to slip beneath the elastic waistband of her shorts.

The husky laugh he gave when he discovered that her knickers were drenched with her arousal reverberated through her, and the drumbeat of desire in her blood beat insistently. She lifted her hips towards his seeking fingers, her whole being focused on her need for him to touch her intimately. And when he did, when he parted her and eased his finger a few centimetres into her slick heat, she gave a low cry.

'*Theos*, you are incredible,' he said thickly. 'I knew that beneath your cool refinement there was fire and passion.' In a deft movement he tugged her shorts and panties down her legs. Her shyness disappeared beneath the fierce glitter in Andreas's eyes as he stared at the cluster of neatly trimmed golden curls at the junction of her thighs.

She almost stopped breathing when he put his hand between her legs and skimmed his fingertips over her sensitive inner thigh, heightening her sense of anticipation as he moved inexorably higher. Finally he rubbed his thumb over her moist opening before pushing a finger into her, deeper than he'd done moments earlier. Her internal muscles immediately clenched and he gave a low laugh as he withdrew his finger a little way and then slid deep once more, in and out, again and again. All the time he kept his eyes locked on her face.

Nothing had prepared her for the swift, shattering orgasm that tensed her muscles as he held her there at the edge for frantic seconds, before he rubbed his thumb over her clitoris and she shuddered and pressed herself harder against his hand.

It had to be a dream, Isla thought when she opened her eyes and saw the filmy white drapes around the bed and the golden lamplight shining through them. It had to be a dream, because in her dreams Andreas had looked at her as he was doing now, with a hunger in his gaze that made her heart leap into her throat.

'You'll stay?' he asked thickly.

Her tongue cleaved to the roof of her mouth as she understood the real question he was asking. Her heart was thudding so hard she was surprised he couldn't hear it. She knew she was ready for her first sexual experience but it was a step too far to articulate her need. She nodded, and Andreas leaned over her and claimed her mouth in a slow, drugging kiss that made Isla tremble as anticipation coiled in her belly.

She watched him strip off his clothes, and the sight of his powerful erection sent a flicker of doubt through her. She was stunned by Andreas's rampant masculinity and it belatedly occurred to her that she should tell him how inexperienced she was. But if she did, he might stop. Even worse, he might be amused to learn that she was still a virgin at her age. Perhaps he would demand to know why she'd chosen him to be her first lover, and Isla had no answer to that, at least not a logical one. Her sense that she and Andreas were destined to be together would likely horrify him as much as it confused her.

He opened the bedside drawer, took a condom out of the packet and rolled it down his thick length.

'I…' Her words died away when he moved over her and claimed her lips in a blatantly erotic kiss that scattered her thoughts. Maybe he sensed her doubts and he lifted his mouth from hers and rested his forehead against her brow.

'If you want to change your mind you have thirty seconds to say so,' he growled.

Her brain urged caution but her body clamoured for his possession. The pleasure he'd induced with his fingers had left her wanting more. After years of suppressing her sensuality she had opened Pandora's Box and released her hungry desire that demanded appeasement. She could feel the swollen tip of Andreas's manhood press against her opening and her instincts took over and she spread her legs wide. 'I haven't changed my mind,' she whispered. 'But I need...'

'I know, *moro mou*. I need this too,' Andreas muttered. And then it was too late for her to explain what she needed to tell him. He lowered himself onto her and his erection was big and hard, stretching her as he pushed forwards and thrust his way into her.

Isla had been prepared for pain, but the pinching sensation between her legs was sharper than she'd expected and she drew an audible breath. Almost instantly the pain faded and there was simply a wonderful sense of him filling her—filling her until she could not say where she ended and he began. A complete union—their two bodies joined as one, she thought dazedly as she opened her eyes and met Andreas's furious gaze.

CHAPTER SIX

'WHY DIDN'T YOU tell me?' Andreas's jaw tensed as he
stared at Isla's flushed face. She blinked and the dreamy
expression in her eyes was replaced with a wariness
that added to his sense of guilt. But damn it, she was
a beautiful, sensual woman and he would never have
guessed that she was a virgin.

He'd accepted her explanation that she and Stelios
were not lovers. Isla had been grieving for her mother
and had sought comfort with Stelios, who she had remembered from when he'd briefly been a father figure to her during her childhood. Nevertheless, Andreas
hadn't intended for things to go as far as having sex
with Isla tonight. He grimaced. Who was he kidding?
he asked himself derisively. He'd wanted her since the
day they'd met.

That kiss in London had blown his mind and he'd
been unable to forget her. Even more unsettling was
the realisation that his reaction to her was not only on
a physical level. He had no idea why he'd told her personal stuff about his difficult relationship with his par-

ents, which he'd never spoken about to anyone before. It was inexplicable that he felt a deeper connection to Isla. The startling discovery that he was her first lover should have appalled him and he did not understand why he felt a possessiveness that was alien to him.

After his conversation with her in the library he had left the party and headed down to the cottage so that he wouldn't be tempted to go to her bedroom at the villa. When he'd seen her walking towards him on the beach he'd decided that fate was helping him out.

'I thought you might stop if I admitted it was my first time.' She shifted beneath him as if she was seeking a more comfortable position. Andreas began to withdraw but hesitated when she stared at him with emotion-filled eyes that set alarm bells ringing in his mind. 'Are you going to stop?'

The rippling effect of her internal muscles around his shaft tested his self-control. 'Do you want me to?' he growled. *Theos*, she was so tight and hot. Sweat beaded his brow as he tried to think about anything other than the fact that he was buried deep inside Isla. But he could smell the erotic scent of her arousal, and when she moved again, arching her hips experimentally, he felt as though he would explode.

'No.'

'No?' For a moment he thought she didn't want him to continue and he forced himself to start to pull back, but she wrapped her legs around his hips.

'Don't stop.' The faintly pleading note in her voice

made him forget that having sex with her was a bad idea. There were rules he would expect her to abide by, and having no expectations of him was at the top of the list.

'Fine, but you need to understand...' He wondered why he'd ever thought her grey eyes were cool. They gleamed like silver rings surrounding the mysterious black pools of her dilated pupils. He was distracted by her lush mouth and his urgency to crush her lips beneath his.

Andreas tried to marshal his thoughts. Isla needed to understand that sex was all he was offering. If he'd known she was a virgin he would have sent her back to the villa, but now it was too late for regrets or recriminations. They would come later. But his biggest regret was that he'd hurt her and the least he could do now was show her just how pleasurable sex could be and make her first experience one that she would never forget.

Isla released her breath when Andreas sank between her thighs so that his erection pushed deeper inside her. She had steeled herself for his rejection when he'd discovered she was a virgin. Her conscience pricked that she should have been honest with him. He had been shocked and angry, but his body was still joined with hers and now he began to move carefully, pulling back a little way and pushing forwards in a rocking motion that made her gasp as the ache inside her grew more intense.

He bent his head to her breast and drew her nipple

into his mouth, sending starbursts of sensation shooting through her as he sucked the stiff peak. By the time he transferred his attention to her other nipple she was breathless and trembling. Molten heat swept through her and burned fiercest at her feminine core as Andreas maintained a steady pace, every thrust of his powerful body claiming her at a primitive level, reinforcing the message that she was his and his alone.

'Touch me,' he muttered. 'I want to feel your hands on me.' The rasp of his voice set her nerve endings alight and his intent expression, as if he was only just hanging onto his control, made her wonder what it would be like if that iron control of his cracked.

She explored his body with her hands, delighting in the feel of his satiny skin beneath her fingertips. She traced a path down his long back to the cleft at the base of his spine while he moved rhythmically up and down, each thrust of his shaft inside her taking her higher. When she dug her nails into his buttocks he swore softly. 'Keep doing that, *omorfia mou,* and this will be over embarrassingly quickly.'

Could she really do that to him? She felt a thrill of feminine power as she pressed her face into his neck and nipped him with her teeth. His skin tasted of salt and sweat. He said something in Greek and bent his head to kiss her hard on her mouth.

'Witch.' He slid his hands beneath her bottom and angled her so that when he drove into her it felt deeper and more intense. At the same time he increased his pace, each stroke faster and harder than the one before. Isla stared at his face, at his clenched jaw and the fierce glitter beneath his heavy lids. There was something savage and untamed about him, no tenderness in the way he gripped her hips and plunged into her with devastating authority.

She felt a frisson of unease as the reality of what she was doing hit her. Andreas was all but a stranger, yet she was lying beneath him and allowing him to take astonishing liberties with her body. Not *allowing* but *relishing*, Isla amended with stark honesty. She loved what he was doing to her. The friction he was creating with every bold thrust was building to a crescendo, and now there was a new urgency in his relentless strokes that made her cling to his sweat-damp shoulders while he drove her towards some unknown place that hovered frustratingly out of reach.

And then, with shocking suddenness, she reached the peak, her body quivering as he held her there for timeless seconds before he drove into her a final time. 'Now,' he said harshly. His body was tense and his jaw clenched as if he was fighting an unstoppable force that overwhelmed him. The primitive groan he made as he climaxed increased Isla's excitement.

She cried out as her orgasm tore through her, causing her internal muscles to spasm, to clench and release over and over again. The pleasure was indescribable and utterly addictive. The tiny part of her brain that was still functioning warned her that Andreas had spoilt her for any other man. Her body had been fashioned for this, for *him,* and as the ripples slowly faded, leaving her limp and spent, she buried her face in his neck and felt the thunder of his heart echo the frantic thud of her own.

Her eyes drifted closed and her muscles relaxed. In a minute she would move away from him, she told herself. But it was beguiling to lie here in his arms and feel safe from the storm.

Andreas woke to find that he was lying on his stomach with his arms tucked beneath his head. His body ached pleasurably and he had never felt such a sense of completeness. Sex with Isla had been off the scale, but he'd known it would be. He hadn't expected her to be a virgin, but her sensuality had blown his mind.

He rolled onto his back and watched thin strips of sunlight slant through the slats of the shutters and make shadow stripes on the rumpled sheet. His sense of well-being faded a little when he discovered that Isla was no longer lying beside him. Last night she had fallen asleep in his arms and she hadn't stirred when he'd untangled himself from her with a reluctance that made him frown as he remembered it. He'd intended to wake her and escort her back to the villa, but the feel of her warm body curled up against him had been dangerously addictive and he must have fallen asleep.

He listened for sounds in the cottage to indicate her whereabouts but all he could hear was the mewing of the gulls outside. She was probably on the beach. Perhaps she'd woken first and hadn't wanted to disturb him, unaware that he would be more than happy to have early morning sex. His erection throbbed as he visualised her gorgeous body.

Before he'd fallen asleep, Andreas had acknowledged that his desire for Isla would not be satisfied by spending one night with her. He wanted her as his mistress. Obviously, she would break off her engagement to his father. Stelios must have believed that he was acting chivalrously when he'd met the daughter of his English mistress and wanted to take care of Isla by offering her a home with him.

Andreas swung his legs over the side of the bed and pulled on his boxer shorts before crossing the room to open the shutters. His mind moved ahead and he considered taking Isla to California and setting her up in an apartment. But he wouldn't want to live with her, or risk her thinking that their affair might lead to a meaningful relationship. He did not do commitment. It might be better to buy her a flat in London where he could visit her regularly so that he retained control of the situation, he mused.

He opened the window and scanned the beach, feeling irritated when there was no sign of her. He knew without conceit that he was a good lover and women were not usually in a rush to leave his bed. Shading his eyes from the bright sun with his hand, he spotted a figure in the distance and recognised Dinos running along the beach towards the cottage.

'*Andreas,* come quickly. Your father...'

Andreas glanced at his watch and cursed as he remembered that he had agreed to meet Stelios in his study at nine a.m. It was ten past. Yesterday his father had said that he had something important to tell him, but hadn't given any clues to what it might be.

The butler reached the cottage and bent over, gasping for breath. Andreas guessed that Isla had gone back to the villa and he felt an inexplicable tug beneath his breastbone that she had gone without saying a word. Before his meeting with Stelios he needed a shower and a gallon of coffee, he decided.

'Will you explain to my father that I overslept, and I'll meet him in fifteen minutes?' he told Dinos.

The butler made a choked sound. 'Kyrios Stelios is...*dead*. I discovered him when I delivered his coffee and newspaper to his room this morning. I knew immediately that something was wrong and I went to wake Miss Stanford.'

Andreas could have sworn that his heart stopped beating for several seconds. He felt as if he had been winded and he snatched a breath to drag oxygen into his lungs. Dinos's words did not make sense. Stelios wasn't dead. It had to be a mistake.

He stared at the butler, shocked to see tears in the older man's eyes. Dinos had worked for the Karelis family for decades. But it couldn't be true. His brain refused to believe it. 'Was Isla in her room?' In the midst of his confusion Andreas wondered when she had returned to the villa.

Dinos gave him an odd look. 'Yes, of course. Miss Stanford was asleep and I woke her and told her that Stelios was unconscious. She remembered that one of your sister's friends who attended the party is a junior doctor. I hurried to find the medic, and he...' Dinos's voice cracked '...he came and pronounced your father dead. The junior doctor is of the opinion that he suffered a heart attack. Stelios's own physician has been summoned from Athens.' Dinos wrung his hands. 'I am so sorry to have to break this terrible news to you, Andreas.'

A heart attack. Andreas's blood froze in his veins. 'My father did not suffer from a heart condition.' He stared at the butler. 'Did he?' The truth was that Dinos was more likely to have known about any health issues Stelios might have had than he was, he thought, feeling a stab of guilt. His father had never confided in him.

'I do not think so.' Dinos hesitated. 'Miss Stanford mentioned to the junior doctor that your father was suffering from cancer. It would be better to talk to her.'

Andreas was unable to process this latest shock. 'I intend to,' he said grimly. He strode back inside the cottage and pulled on the rest of his clothes, feeling numb. Dinos had started to walk back to the villa when Andreas sprinted past the older man. But it made no difference how fast he ran. He was too late to say to his father all the things that he wished he'd said.

* * *

It was early evening when Andreas strode out of his father's study and noticed a suitcase in the entrance hall. All the guests who had attended Nefeli's birthday party had left the island hours ago, and he had spent much of the day trying to comfort his distraught sister. A press statement had been released announcing Stelios Karelis's unexpected death. But it had not been unexpected by his father, Andreas brooded. Stelios had chosen to keep the news that he had terminal cancer a secret from his family, and only his doctors and one other person had been in his confidence.

He walked into the lounge and silently cursed the clench of his heart when he saw Isla standing by the window. The navy blue dress she was wearing was starkly plain and her hair fell in a long plait down her back, but a lack of adornments only accentuated her classical beauty. She appeared to be absorbed in the view of the garden but he sensed she was lost in her thoughts. That idea was strengthened when she visibly jumped as he halted beside her.

'Andreas, I didn't hear you.' She was pale but composed, always, he thought darkly, shoving away memories of how she had looked in the throes of her orgasm, her face flushed and her eyes wide with surprise and pleasure. She reached out and touched his arm in a brief show of sympathy, he supposed, but the light brush of her hand across his skin felt as if she'd branded him. 'I'm so sorry,' she whispered.

'Why didn't you tell me that my father was dying?' he demanded. He'd felt a hollow sensation inside him as he'd stared at Stelios's body and seen the signs of illness that he'd missed when the old man was alive because his attention had been distracted by Isla.

'He asked me not to. He intended to tell you and Nefeli after her party.' She sighed. 'Your father learned a few months ago that his cancer was incurable and he chose to stop having treatment which could only delay the inevitable for a short time. But he was determined that nothing would spoil Nefeli's twenty-first birthday.'

Isla twisted her hands together and Andreas noted that she was no longer wearing her diamond engagement ring. 'Stelios asked me to pretend to be his fiancée to divert attention away from him,' she said. 'He had lost weight and was often tired, but he thought no one would notice the signs of his illness if he announced his intention to marry a much younger woman.'

She was silent for a moment and tears shimmered in her eyes. 'I don't know if he was aware that chemotherapy had weakened his heart. He never mentioned anything to me. But during the party he said he felt breathless.' Her voice dropped to a whisper. 'If I had done something then, persuaded him to call a doctor...'

Emotions that Andreas had held back all day while he'd taken care of his sister and dealt with the numerous arrangements that needed to be made clogged his throat. 'It's doubtful that you or anyone else could have prevented what happened,' he said gruffly. 'I have re-

ceived word from the hospital in Athens where my father's body was taken. A post-mortem confirmed that
he suffered a massive heart attack and death would have
been instantaneous.'

He glanced over at the drinks cabinet but resisted
the urge to pour himself a stiff Scotch. Nothing could
anaesthetise the dull ache in his chest which was made
worse by the knowledge that his father had confided
in Isla but not in *him*. It apparently counted for nothing
that he was Stelios's son and heir. At least he presumed
he would succeed his father as head of Karelis Corp.
The family's lawyer, John Sabanis, was on his way to
Louloudi to reveal the terms of Stelios's will.

'You *should* have told me,' he said curtly. '*Theos*,
you let me believe that you were my father's fiancée.'

'You accused me of being a gold-digger.' The sting
in her voice was unexpected and, even though he deserved her scorn, Andreas frowned.

'What was I supposed to think? My father brought
you here to Louloudi and introduced you as the woman
he intended to marry, despite the fact that you are young
enough to have been his daughter.'

'And you were jealous because you wanted me,' she
said flatly, coming too close to a truth he did not want
to admit to. Isla had insisted that her loyalty to Stelios
had prevented her from explaining the truth about her
relationship with him. But had her actions been entirely
altruistic, as she claimed? Andreas wondered cynically.

'Why did you agree to a fake engagement with my father? Did he offer to pay you?'

'Of course not,' she said angrily. 'I've told you I was very fond of Stelios after he had been kind to me when I was a child. When he was diagnosed with cancer I took care of him.'

From outside the window came the sound of the helicopter. 'That will be my lift to the mainland,' she muttered. 'Dinos has arranged for me to be flown to Athens. I've booked a hotel room for tonight and a flight to London in the morning.'

'You don't have to leave right away.' Andreas could not explain why the hollow feeling inside him expanded at the idea of Isla leaving. He was still in shock at Stelios's death. His throat felt tight as he sought to suppress emotions that he'd denied he was capable of feeling for most of his life. He had cultivated an image of a carefree playboy so successfully that he'd almost believed it was who he was, all he was capable of being. Right now he felt raw and out of control when he thought about his failings as a son and his complicated relationship with his father.

Isla was looking at him with concern in her grey eyes, as if she understood what he was going through, as if she cared. He told himself that he did not want her compassion. What he wanted was much more basic. The only human interaction he really understood was sex, and he wanted to be inside her, to trace his hands over her satiny skin and sink between her pale thighs, allow pleasure to blot out for a few moments the pain that had lodged like a bur in his chest.

He watched her eyes darken, the pupils enlarging until the irises were thin rims of silver. Her tongue darted over her bottom lip and the emptiness inside Andreas became a huge, all-encompassing ache that he assured himself was nothing more than desire. He lifted his hand and ran his finger lightly down her cheek. Her skin had the texture of a velvety peach. He felt the tremor that ran through her and the idea that he affected her as much as she affected him made him feel slightly better. They were both prisoners of this crazy passion—crazy was the only word that came anywhere close to describing the thunder of his heart when Isla swayed towards him.

'Stay,' he said thickly. When she shook her head he clasped her shoulders and pulled her towards him. 'We could start over, without any misunderstandings this time.'

Her expression was unguarded and faintly wistful. 'Do you want to?'

He wanted *her*, which wasn't quite the same thing. Andreas ignored his conscience and moved his hand down to cup her bottom, his heart kicking in his chest as she gave a low moan when he hauled her against him.

'Does this give you an idea of what I want, *omorfia mou*?' he murmured before he angled his mouth over hers.

CHAPTER SEVEN

'ANDREAS—KYRIOS SABANIS has arrived…' Dinos halted in the doorway of the lounge and looked uncomfortable when Isla jerked out of Andreas's arms. He swore silently as he stared at her expressive features and watched her barriers go up. The butler's timing was terrible, but his own wasn't great, he conceded. His father had been dead for less than twenty-four hours and he was the only person who knew that Stelios's engagement to Isla had been fake.

'I should go. You will be busy with arrangements and things…' Isla avoided his gaze and walked quickly across the room. Dinos stepped aside as Andreas followed her into the hallway.

'At least tell me the name of your hotel in Athens…' He broke off abruptly and hid his frustration when his father's lawyer heaved himself up from a chair.

'Andreas, this is a dreadful day,' John Sabanis said, extending his hand. 'Isla, you have my deepest sympathy.'

'Thank you, John.' Catching Andreas's puzzled look,

she explained, 'John and I met on several occasions when he visited your father's house in London.'

The portly lawyer nodded. 'Stelios's death will be a shock to many people. Despite his age, he was in the prime of his life, which was demonstrated when he announced his engagement to you, Isla. I could not help but overhear that you intend to leave Louloudi.'

She did not look at Andreas. 'Yes, Andreas and Nefeli need privacy.'

'It would be better if you delay your departure until after I have explained the terms of Stelios's will,' the lawyer said.

'Is that really necessary? You are aware that I witnessed the will you drew up for Stelios last year, which means that I cannot be a beneficiary.'

'Stelios recently made a new will.' John Sabanis looked at Andreas. 'You asked me here because you want to know who your father chose to succeed him as Chairman of Karelis Corp. I suggest that we discuss your father's last will and testament without further delay.'

'We'll go into the study.' Andreas opened the door and ushered the lawyer into the room.

Isla glanced towards the stairs and, following her gaze, Andreas saw his sister run across the hall.

'I'm surprised you are still here, Isla,' Nefeli said sharply. 'I thought you would already be looking for your next wealthy old man to sink your talons into.'

'There is no need for rudeness,' Andreas murmured.

His sister was headstrong but she had been much closer to their father and her eyes were red-rimmed from crying. As yet he hadn't found the right moment to explain that Stelios's engagement to Isla had been an elaborate pretence.

'Why are you defending her? What's going on?' Nefeli demanded.

'John Sabanis is here to read Papa's will and he has asked Isla to be present.'

Nefeli glowered at Isla before she marched into the study and threw herself down onto the sofa. With obvious reluctance Isla walked into the room and perched on a chair close to the door. Andreas's phone pinged for what seemed like the millionth time and he frowned when he saw numerous messages from the COO of Karelis Corp, saying that they needed to talk urgently. Not now, he thought grimly as he switched his phone setting to silent.

The lawyer sat down at the desk and took a sheaf of documents from his briefcase. 'I will hand out copies of Stelios's will which he signed three days ago, on the fourteenth of September, so that you can read it at your own leisure. But to summarise—it was Stelios's wish that his son Andreas should succeed him in the joint roles of Chairman and CEO of Karelis Corporation, with the full backing of the board.'

It was what Andreas had expected. The sole reason for his existence as far as his parents had been concerned was so that he could step into his father's shoes and run the company with the same single-minded devotion to business that Stelios had shown. In due course he would make an advantageous marriage with the aim of producing the next Karelis heir. These things he would do, Andreas vowed to himself. He had not been the son Stelios had hoped for when he was alive, but he would honour his father in death by accepting his duty and doing his best to fulfil the old man's expectations.

The responsibility of his position was sinking in and it felt as if a heavy weight had settled on his shoulders. He had assumed that his father would live for many more years and the handover of power would have been a gradual process. He listened as the lawyer ran through various bequests Stelios had made to members of the extended Karelis family and some of the staff.

Dinos and Toula were to receive the deeds of the staff cottage attached to the villa which had been their home for many years. The bulk of Stelios's personal fortune, including the family home in Athens and the house in London, was split between Andreas and a trust fund for Nefeli which she could access on her twenty-fifth birthday.

'Why can't I have my money now?' Nefeli said sulkily.

'Your father was concerned that you would be the target of fortune hunters,' John Sabanis explained. 'You are one of the richest women in Europe but for the next few years Andreas will be in charge of your trust fund for your own protection.'

The lawyer cleared his throat. 'Finally, we come to the matter of Louloudi. It was Stelios's wish that ownership of the island, including the villa, will be shared equally between his son Andreas and Miss Isla Stanford.'

Andreas's jaw clenched. It was a trait he had perfected, allowing him to disguise his true feelings, which right now were a mix of incomprehension and fury. There were few things he cared deeply about but Louloudi had been his boyhood playground and it was the only place where he had spent any quality time with his father. Stelios's decision to bequeath fifty per cent ownership of Louloudi to Isla felt like the ultimate betrayal.

Nefeli leapt up. 'Papa *can't* have intended to give away Louloudi, which has been owned by the Karelis family for three generations, to his English tart. He must have been coerced into writing a new will.' She threw Isla a poisonous look. 'It was Papa who needed protection from a fortune hunter.'

Andreas exhaled heavily. 'The situation between Papa and Isla was not as it seemed. Stelios asked Isla to pretend to be his fiancée because he knew he was terminally ill and he wanted to keep the news from you until after your party.'

'Did Papa tell you that?'

'No, Isla explained everything.'

'And you believe her frankly suspicious story? What does Isla have that makes sane men lose their minds?'

Nefeli said scathingly. 'I saw how you pawed her when you danced with her at my party. Men are such idiots.'

Guilt churned in the pit of Andreas's stomach. He should have paid more attention to his father, who had looked tired and old. But he'd barely registered Stelios's physical decline because he'd been obsessed with Isla. Something hard and cold congealed inside him when he remembered his mother's obsessive feelings for Stelios and her bitter unhappiness when she'd realised that he did not love her.

It was the reason why Andreas deliberately avoided relationships that required an emotional response from him. He had no intention of ever falling in love. Isla had overstepped the boundaries when she'd failed to tell him she was a virgin. He hoped she did not think there had been anything romantic about the night they had spent together because he certainly didn't.

She stood up and gave him a faintly pleading look. 'I did not coerce your father to include me in his will. The opposite, in fact. I made it clear to him that I didn't want him to leave me a bequest. I had no idea that he planned to make me a joint owner of the island.'

Andreas glanced at John Sabanis. 'When did my father decide to make a new will?'

'He phoned me a few days ago and requested that I meet him here on Louloudi,' the lawyer said. 'Following the news of Stelios's engagement to Isla, I was not surprised that he wanted to make provision for her in the event of his death, although I was not aware that he was suffering from incurable cancer.'

'My father chose to only confide in Isla,' Andreas said tersely.

'I refuse to accept the bequest Stelios left me.' Isla turned to John Sabanis. 'Louloudi should remain in the ownership of the Karelis family.'

'Actually, you cannot refuse it.' The lawyer shrugged. 'Like it or not, a fifty per cent share of the island will be held in trust for you for one year. After that you can sell your share but you must offer it to Andreas first, and it cannot be sold for less than its market value. The current value of Louloudi is one hundred million euros.'

Isla gasped and John Sabanis gave her a wry look before he continued. 'But you and Andreas must both return to the island on the first anniversary of Stelios's death and live here for one month. If either of you fails to carry out the terms of the will, then ownership of Louloudi will pass entirely to the other person.'

'Clearly my father thought it would be amusing to play games from beyond the grave,' Andreas growled. 'He can't have been of sound mind when he set out those ridiculous terms. There must be grounds to challenge the will.'

John shook his head. 'Stelios was completely sane and it was his right to dispose of his assets as he wished.'

Nefeli ran across the study and opened the door. She spun round and glared at Isla. 'You poisoned my father's mind.'

'I promise you that I didn't.' Isla hurried out of the room after the young Greek woman.

'Leave her,' Andreas advised when he followed Isla into the entrance hall. 'My sister is still in shock.'

'I wish this hadn't happened,' she said in a low voice. 'I'm as stunned as you are by the terms of your father's will.'

He raked a hand through his hair. 'You can't lose, can you, Isla? You know I'll do anything to regain complete ownership of Louloudi and in a year from now I will have to buy your share.'

'If I don't return next year and live here for a month, then I will forfeit my share of the island.'

'But you will come back.' He gave a weary smile when she shook her head. 'Of course you will. You stand to inherit a fortune.'

Andreas wondered if Stelios had written his will as revenge because many years ago he'd forced his father to choose between his family in Greece and his English mistress. Isla was certain that Stelios had been in love with her mother. When Stelios had learned that his cancer was incurable, he'd made sure that the daughter of the woman he had loved would be provided for.

Love made fools of people, Andreas thought darkly. His mother had been so desperate to win Stelios's affection that she'd had no time or love for her son. What he felt for Isla was lust, nothing more, he assured himself. Yet he could not bring himself to step away from her.

'I'm sorry I couldn't tell you about your father's illness.'

'Couldn't?' He gave an angry laugh. 'You slept with me but still you said nothing.'

'My loyalty was to Stelios.'

Her words felt as if she'd shoved a knife between his ribs. 'And yet you gave your virginity to me. Why did you leave the cottage without waking me this morning?'

'I thought it would be less awkward for both of us.' She bit her lower lip and Andreas could not tear his eyes from her lush mouth. 'I can't stay here,' she whispered. 'Your sister is upset.'

'I'm hardly thrilled that Stelios left you a chunk of my birthright,' he said sardonically.

'Do you think I persuaded him to write that will?'

'I don't know what to think.' Andreas looked away from the hurt expression in Isla's eyes. His gut told him that she had spoken the truth, but for the sake of his sanity he needed to distance himself from her. He tensed when she stepped closer and he breathed in her evocative perfume.

'Your father loved you,' she said gently. Rising up on her toes, she brushed her mouth over his cheek and Andreas's breath became trapped in his lungs. He knew that if he turned his head a fraction, Isla's lips would meet his. But if he allowed her to kiss his mouth he did not trust himself to resist kissing her back. He wanted so much more than a kiss from this woman, who fascinated him more than any woman had ever done. And so he forced himself to remain rigid, his mouth a firm line of defence against her sweetly sensual onslaught.

After a few seconds that felt to Andreas like a life-time, Isla lifted her lips from his cheek and gave a soft sigh before she turned away and walked across the hall. Her suitcase was no longer by the front door and he guessed that the pilot had taken it to the helicopter.

She opened the door and stepped outside. He wanted to call her back, go after her. Instead he clenched his hands by his sides when she closed the door behind her with a quiet click that was somehow more dramatic, more final than if she'd slammed it shut. Minutes later came the sound of the helicopter taking off.

'Andreas—' John Sabanis spoke from the study doorway '—you need to see this.'

The phone in Andreas's pocket vibrated constantly as new messages came in. Cursing beneath his breath, he strode into the study and stared at a live newsfeed on the computer screen.

Greece's largest petroleum company Karelis Corp is facing a hostile takeover bid from the French firm Moulet Energie, which has announced that it is near to acquiring a majority interest in Kare-lis Corp's stock.

'What the hell?' As soon as he switched his phone set-ting from silent it started to ring, and the nightmare began.

It *couldn't* be true! Isla's legs gave way and she sank down onto the edge of the bath, staring at the pregnancy test in her hand. *Positive*. But how? Andreas had used protection the one and only time they'd had sex.

She choked back a sob as she remembered how she had hoped day after day that he would contact her when she'd left Louloudi. He had been busy dealing with major problems at Karelis Corp, she'd reminded herself. But as weeks passed and she did not hear from him, her sense of hurt had deepened. She had given Andreas her virginity but his silence made it clear that he had only wanted a one-night stand—and now she was expecting his baby.

Her stomach lurched at the thought that she did not even have anywhere to live. She had returned to Stelios's house in Kensington in the vain hope that Andreas would come to her. But she'd received a letter from his lawyer informing her that the house was being sold and she must vacate the property.

Isla tried to curb her sense of panic. Her period was late—very late—and she'd been feeling under the weather for weeks, but she'd bought a pregnancy test not really believing that her suspicion could be true. The blue line on the test stared back at her. She was ten weeks into her pregnancy but the risk of miscarriage was higher in the first trimester. Maybe there wouldn't be a baby.

Her hand moved involuntarily to her stomach as if she could protect the tiny life she carried within her. In that moment she knew without a shadow of doubt that she wanted her baby. Her pregnancy was not planned but the baby would be loved unconditionally by his or her mother at least. But what about Andreas? How would he react to the news that he was going to be a father?

'Isla, are you going to be long in there? I need to leave for work soon,' Beth called out from the other side of the bathroom door. Isla jumped up and shoved the pregnancy test in the bin. Her best friend from university had allowed her to sleep on the sofa in her tiny flat for the past few weeks while she'd been flat-hunting. Rents in the capital were high and she was struggling to find somewhere she could afford. How was she going to manage when she had a baby? She couldn't do this alone, she realised. But maybe, hopefully, she would have Andreas's support.

She opened the door and forced a smile for her friend. 'Sorry.'

'I heard you being sick again this morning,' Beth said, grabbing her toothbrush and standing over the sink.

'I must have picked up a stomach bug.' Isla followed Beth's gaze to the box that the pregnancy test had been in, which she'd forgotten to throw away.

'Oh, God, Isla.' Toothpaste squirted from the tube in Beth's hand and landed on the floor. 'What are you going to do?'

Tears blurred her vision. 'I don't know,' she admitted shakily. She wondered if her mum had felt the same sense of dread when she'd faced having to break the news to Isla's father that she was pregnant. What if Andreas did not want his child, just as David Stanford hadn't wanted his daughter? There was only one way to find out.

'There is a Miss Isla Stanford in Reception asking to see you. I've explained that your diary is full but she says she won't leave.' Andreas's PA sounded irritated. 'Do you want me to call Security?'

Holding the phone to his ear, he drummed the fingers of his other hand on the desk. He was seriously tempted to send Isla away but he could not deny he was curious about why she had come to Athens. It was two months since he'd last seen her on Louloudi, and lately he'd stopped thinking about her quite so much. But that was only because his workload was so crazy that he didn't have time to think about anything other than trying to save Karelis Corp, Andreas acknowledged grimly. At night it was a different matter and Isla invaded his dreams with annoying regularity.

Was she hoping for a repeat performance of the night they had spent together? He pictured her naked, supple body—her breasts that fitted into his palms as if they had been made for that purpose, and her long slender legs that she'd wrapped around his hips when he'd possessed her. His body clenched hard and he cursed beneath his breath.

'Show Miss Stanford to my office,' he told Daphne.

'Your meeting with the Dutch client, Mr Vanek, is in fifteen minutes,' his PA reminded him.

'This won't take long.' He'd made the decision when Isla had left Louloudi that he would not get involved with her. He would discover the purpose of her visit and then send her away, he assured himself. He walked over to the window that overlooked the Karelis refinery, one of the largest and most modern oil refineries in Europe. Although how long it would continue to be owned by Karelis Corp was the subject of much speculation in the business world and the media, Andreas thought with a grimace. Beyond the tangle of metal pipes and towers the Aegean Sea sparkled beneath the pale winter sun.

He was aware of his heart thumping in his chest and his inexplicable reaction to the prospect of meeting Isla again infuriated him. He heard his office door open, followed by the soft click of it closing again. But he did not immediately turn around until he was confident that he had himself under control.

'Hello, Andreas.'

Isla's cool voice did nothing to put out the fire raging inside him when he swung round and stared at her. She was even more beautiful than he remembered. A little thinner perhaps, and her face was paler now that the golden tan she'd had in Greece two months ago had faded. But there was something about her—a glow as if she was lit from within—that Andreas could not explain. She looked mouth-watering in tight-fitting jeans and a smoky grey jumper that matched the colour of her eyes.

He clenched his hands by his sides, fighting an urge to stride across the room, pull her into his arms and kiss her until they were both senseless. Somehow he managed to sound politely uninterested. 'Isla, this is a surprise,' he drawled.

'Is it?' Colour flared on her cheeks and he did not miss the bite in her tone. 'We were lovers. Does that mean nothing to you?'

He dismissed the erotic memories that barged un-asked for into his mind, and shoved his hands into his trouser pockets to disguise the evidence of his desire. With another woman he might have instigated an affair, but not with Isla. She was the only woman who had threatened his self-control and he would not allow it to happen again. 'We had sex once. Take my advice and don't look for romance where none exists,' he told her.

She gave an odd laugh. 'Once is all it takes.'

His eyes narrowed. 'What do you mean?' He frowned when she did not reply and strode over to stand in front of her. Instantly he knew it had been a bad move as he breathed in her perfume and felt a throb in his groin. *Theos*, this woman made him feel like a teenager with an overload of hormones. He made a show of checking his watch. 'I have a business meeting scheduled and I'd allocated you five minutes of my time. You've used three of them.'

Her eyes flashed but there was a vulnerability about

the way her tongue darted nervously over her lips. 'I'm pregnant.'

Andreas rocked back on his heels. He was totally unprepared for the bombshell she'd dropped, and his first thought was, *Not again*. He had been in this situation once before when Sadie had told him she was expecting his child. His response to Isla was the same as it had been to his lying ex-girlfriend. 'I suppose you expect me to believe it's my baby?' he said coldly.

She blinked. 'Of course it's your baby. You know quite well that I was a virgin when I slept with you.'

He nodded. 'Yes, that was convenient. But you could have had other sexual partners in the last two months.'

Twin spots of colour flared on her cheeks. 'Because, having lost my virginity to you, I was filled with uncontrollable lust and had sex with numerous men?' she suggested sarcastically. 'You are the only man I have ever slept with.'

Andreas could not explain the possessiveness that swept through him at the idea that she was exclusively his. 'Why me?' His brows rose. 'You are what, twenty-four or five? Surely you've had boyfriends. Why did you choose me to be your first lover?'

'God knows,' she muttered. 'It must be your charming personality.'

'Or perhaps you were attracted to my wealth,' he said drily. 'How can you possibly be pregnant by me when I used protection?'

'I don't know how it happened. No forms of con-

traception are foolproof and I guess we were just un-
lucky…or lucky—depending on your point of view…'

'Enough.' With an effort Andreas brought his temper under control. 'I don't believe the baby is mine but
I am willing to accept there is a minuscule chance. The
only way I can be certain if you are telling the truth is
with a DNA test.'

The glimmer of tears turned Isla's eyes to the colour of wet slate. 'Do you really think I would lie about
something this important? I *am* telling you the truth.
I'm expecting your child.'

Sadie had used almost exactly the same words and
she had cried prettily too, Andreas thought savagely.
He would be a fool to believe Isla. He should tell her
to contact his lawyer so that a paternity test could be
arranged, before calling Security to escort her from
the building. So why was he hesitating? What kind of
witchery had she cast on him that tempted him to pull
her into his arms and reassure her he would take care
of her and the child?

His phone pinged and he read a message informing
him that the Dutch client was waiting in the boardroom.
Coming to a decision, he spoke to his PA and instructed
her to organise some refreshments to be delivered to the
hospitality suite. 'English tea, and some sandwiches,'
he said, his eyes on Isla's slender figure. She did not
look pregnant. Was she eating enough? *Theos*, why did
he care?

Jaw clenching, he looked away from the wounded

look in her eyes. It was highly unlikely that he'd made her pregnant, but he wasn't going to risk her selling a pack of lies to the tabloids like Sadie had done. He would insist that Isla remained in Athens until she'd had a blood test which would prove whether or not he was the father of her child.

'My secretary will take you to the hospitality room,' he told her. 'Wait for me there and we will continue this discussion later.'

It was unfair that Andreas was so handsome, Isla thought bitterly as she watched him stride out of his office. His arrogance infuriated her, but her pulse had raced when he'd stood close to her. She'd stared at his mouth, remembering the beauty of his kiss. The evocative scent of his aftershave lingered in the room after he had gone, evoking images in her mind of his sweat-beaded shoulders, his hair slicked back from his brow and his face contorted with pleasure when he'd climaxed inside her.

She gave an angry sigh. Andreas's reaction to the news of her pregnancy had been even worse than she'd feared. Now he expected her to wait patiently while he was in a meeting. His attitude showed that he thought she was a nuisance who he would have to slot into his busy schedule. She ground her teeth as she remembered how he had accused her of sleeping around. His contemptuous expression when she'd told him that he was her baby's father was something she would never forget.

It reminded her of when she was sixteen and her father, who she had met for the first and only time, had told her that, in his eyes, she did not exist. She'd slunk out of the art gallery where David Stanford had been exhibiting his work. But she'd hesitated in the doorway and looked over her shoulder, hoping even then that her father would call her back and apologise for abandoning her. But he hadn't looked in her direction and she knew he had already forgotten her. The memory still haunted her and she could not bear the idea of her child one day feeling rejected and humiliated by Andreas.

He had made it plain that he did not want his baby. There was no reason for him to demand a paternity test when he knew she had been a virgin. She was damned if she would be forced to prove that she had told him the truth, and Andreas could go to hell.

CHAPTER EIGHT

THE HELICOPTER DIPPED low over an olive grove and the villa came into view. Andreas remembered the excitement he'd felt as a boy coming to Louloudi every summer when his boarding school in England broke up for the holidays. His mother hadn't wanted him at the family home in Athens and he'd been glad to escape from her constant disapproval. Occasionally Stelios had spent a weekend on the island and Andreas had treasured those times that he'd had his father's exclusive attention. But mostly Stelios had been preoccupied with work.

He rubbed his hand over the stubble on his chin. In three days' time it would be the first anniversary of his father's death. For the past year Andreas had fought to save Karelis Corp from being bought out by a rival company. It had been a hellish time and he was mentally exhausted, but at least the company was safe. Now he was determined to save Louloudi from falling into the hands of the most unscrupulous woman he'd ever had the misfortune to meet.

His jaw clenched. Ten months ago Isla had turned

up at his office in Athens and announced that she was pregnant. Not unreasonably, he'd demanded proof of paternity before he would accept responsibility for the child she alleged was his. But her tears had stirred his conscience and he had asked himself why she would lie. It couldn't be because she needed financial support for her child. Stelios had made provision for her in his will and she was due to inherit a fortune. Andreas had needed time to think, but when his meeting with a client had finished and he'd gone to find Isla, his PA informed him that she had already left.

He'd felt responsible for her, despite his suspicion that the child wasn't his, and he had instructed his security team to search for her, to no avail. She had seemingly disappeared into thin air. The fact that she had not contacted him again seemed further proof that if she had been pregnant it wasn't his child, Andreas brooded as he climbed out of the helicopter and walked across the lawn towards the house.

But he did not doubt that she would turn up on Louloudi to claim her inheritance. She wasn't going to miss the chance to become a multi-millionaire and he would have to bite the bullet and buy her share of the island. He was confident that the powerful attraction he'd felt for her would have died. He had dated a few women, although he hadn't had sex for a year. But he'd assumed that his lack of libido was down to his excessive workload. It was not because he subconsciously compared every woman he met to Isla, he assured himself.

He strode into the house and his vision was momentarily obscured while the lenses in his sunglasses transitioned from the bright light outside to the darker interior. He blinked—but the pram parked in the hallway was still there. Shock ricocheted through him until he remembered that Toula and Dinos's daughter had been pregnant. Maria must have brought her new baby to visit its grandparents.

Andreas stepped closer to the pram and saw an infant, he had no idea how old, sleeping peacefully. The blue blanket tucked around the baby suggested it was a boy. He had an olive-gold complexion, a mass of dark hair and impossibly long eyelashes that made crescents on his cheeks. Andreas's heart missed a beat when the baby's lashes lifted to reveal bright blue eyes. The exact shade of blue as his own eyes.

Hadn't he read somewhere that all babies were born with blue eyes? He tried to quell the panic that surged through him. Of course this child could not be his. But he felt strangely reluctant to move away from the pram. The baby was so vulnerable. Perhaps the fierce protectiveness he felt was a normal response to seeing something so small and helpless, he thought. He'd never been this close to a baby before. Some of his friends had children, but he'd pretended to admire the usually squalling infant from a safe distance.

Behind him he heard a door open, followed by a swiftly indrawn breath. 'Andreas! I wasn't expecting you to arrive for a couple of days.'

Even then he did not take his gaze from the baby. He was crazy to believe he could see a resemblance between himself and the infant, and crazier still to feel a connection to the tiny scrap of humanity in the pram. He finally turned his head towards the familiar voice that had stirred something within him which was too complicated to define.

Andreas's breath hissed between his teeth as he stared at Isla. The white cotton shirt she wore tied in a knot at her waist revealed her flat stomach, and skimpy denim shorts showed off her long slender legs. Her honey-gold hair was drawn back from her face in a ponytail and a few tendrils clung to her pink cheeks. Despite the villa's air conditioning, the atmosphere in the entrance hall was sultry and prickled with an electricity that was almost tangible.

'I thought you were in New York.' Her tone was faintly accusing. 'A photo of you and one of your girlfriends who was almost wearing a dress was on the front page of several of the tabloids.'

'You sound jealous, Isla.'

Her flush deepened. 'Yeah, right,' she muttered. 'Your trouble, Andreas, is that you think you're God's gift to womankind.'

'Is that your opinion?' He didn't know why he enjoyed teasing her so that her eyes flashed silver with temper. Andreas refused to question why seeing Isla again made him feel more alive than he'd felt for months.

'You don't want to know what I think of you.'

'Your body is sending out clues,' he murmured, dropping his gaze to the hard points of her nipples jutting beneath her shirt. He laughed softly as she quickly crossed her arms over her breasts.

'It's chilly in here,' she snapped, her tongue darting out to lick a bead of sweat above her top lip.

Andreas was aware of his body's damning reaction. His blood pounded in his ears and his erection pressed uncomfortably against his trousers. So much for his assumption that he would no longer be attracted to Isla. Desire swept like molten lava through his veins and he was desperate to take her to bed. He stepped closer to her and breathed in the delicate floral fragrance of her perfume mixed with another scent that he could not name but reminded him of vanilla.

She did not back away from him and he felt the tremor that shook her slender frame. Her soft pink mouth was a delectable temptation but, as he lowered his head, his body tensing with anticipation of claiming her lips with his, a cry came from the pram, shattering the spell that Isla had cast on him. He jerked back from her and raked a hand through his hair.

'Where is Dinos and Toula's daughter?' Isla looked puzzled, and he growled, 'I assume the baby is Maria's.'

'No. He is mine.' She scooped the infant into her arms and her expression softened. 'It's all right, sweetheart. Mama's here,' she murmured. The look of love in her eyes for her child made her even more beautiful.

'So you weren't lying about being pregnant,' Andreas said curtly.

'I've never lied to you.' She took her gaze from the baby and her eyes glittered. 'Loukas is your son.'

'Like hell he is.' Even as he refuted her claim Andreas recalled the sense of recognition he'd felt when he'd looked into the baby's blue eyes. But it couldn't be true, his brain insisted. 'Why did you disappear from my office after claiming that I was responsible for your pregnancy? And why did you refuse a DNA test?'

'I felt humiliated that you expected me to prove I was telling the truth,' Isla said fiercely. 'You *are* Loukas's father.'

He stared at her, wondering if her cheeks were flushed with anger at his refusal to believe her, or did she feel guilty because she was lying? 'It's not unheard of for women to accuse rich men of fathering their child,' he said sardonically. 'I barely know you, yet you expect me to take your word without any degree of certainty that this is my baby.'

'You can be certain that I was a virgin when I slept with you.' Pride replaced the anger in her voice. She tilted her chin and held his gaze. 'Have you any idea how insulting you are to accuse me of pretending that Loukas is yours for financial reasons? I don't want your money. Stelios made me a beneficiary in his will and I'm not after a maintenance payout from you.'

She played *outraged* very convincingly, but Andreas wanted hard facts before he would be convinced. 'Why would you object to a paternity test unless you are worried that the result will show you are a fantasist?'

Her eyes flashed silver. 'You are unbelievable. Loukas is your son, but I am prepared to raise him on my own. Are you prepared to walk away from your flesh and blood? Think hard before you give me your answer because your decision is final and you can't change your mind in the future if the idea of fatherhood suddenly becomes more appealing.'

The baby started crying in earnest, his little face turning red. It was a heartrending sound that evoked an unexpected emotional response in Andreas. He wanted to reach out and take the baby in his arms to comfort him but Isla turned away and walked across the hall, holding the baby against her shoulder. She paused in the doorway to the lounge and glanced back at Andreas.

'If you refuse to accept that Loukas is your son I will tell him when he is old enough to understand that his father is dead. It will spare him the heartbreak of wondering why you rejected him.'

The bitterness in her voice startled Andreas as much as her ultimatum. He was reeling with shock that quickly turned to anger.

'If you *are* telling the truth why didn't you contact me when you gave birth?' he demanded as he followed her into the room. He found her sitting on the sofa, crooning softly to the baby while she unbuttoned her shirt. The tender expression on her face as she held the baby to her breast evoked an ache in his chest. He wondered if his mother had ever looked at him with such loving affection when he was born. He certainly had no recollection of her doing so when he was older.

The sun streaming through the window picked out the golden strands in Isla's hair as she sat feeding her baby. She seemed to Andreas like the biblical Eve, the first woman and mother but also a temptress who he was determined to resist.

'Can you pass me a muslin? The square of material in the change bag,' she said when he frowned.

Andreas spotted a large colourful bag, opened it and handed Isla a piece of white cloth. 'You need all this equipment for one small baby?' he said in astonishment. The bag contained disposable nappies, feeding bottles, a dummy and various other items that he had no idea what they were for. He put the bag on the coffee table and a red booklet slipped onto the floor.

'It's Loukas's record book for when I have him weighed,' Isla explained as he bent down to retrieve it.

Andreas flicked through the pages and read the baby's date of birth. 'It says here that Loukas was born on the eighteenth of May, which makes him four months old.' His jaw hardened. 'We had sex in mid-September a year ago. If you had conceived my baby then, as you say you did, you should have given birth three months ago, in June.' He gave a cold laugh. 'You appear to have slipped up on rudimentary mathematics, Isla.'

'He was born three weeks early.'

'How convenient,' he drawled. '*Theo*s, what kind of a fool do you take me for?'

Hectic colour stained her cheeks. '*You are such a jerk!* You're so high and mighty, but you are wrong about me. Loukas had to be delivered at thirty-seven weeks because I developed a serious complication with my pregnancy which threatened his life and mine.'

Through her tears Isla saw Andreas's shocked expression and her conscience pricked that she could have been gentler when she'd revealed that their baby had nearly died at birth. But maybe he didn't care, she thought bleakly. She was still traumatised by memories of the routine antenatal appointment when it had been discovered that her blood pressure was sky-high and the baby was showing signs of distress. She had read about pre-eclampsia, but she'd been fit and healthy throughout her pregnancy and hadn't expected to develop a potentially life-threatening complication.

'You have no idea how terrified I was when I was rushed into hospital in an ambulance and immediately prepared for theatre,' she said rawly. 'Loukas's heartbeat was dropping and they had to get him out quickly by caesarean section. He spent the first week of his life in the neonatal intensive care unit and it was touch-and-go if he would survive.'

She brushed her hand across her eyes. 'The worst thing of all was knowing that Loukas was alone while he fought for his life. I was too unwell for a few days after the birth to visit him. Where were you then, Andreas?' she demanded bitterly. 'You failed Loukas when he needed you. I don't know why I thought that there might be a shred of decency in you when I brought him to Louloudi so that you could meet your son.'

Andreas's hard-boned features gave no clue to his thoughts and he did not say another word as he strode out of the room. It was becoming a regular occurrence for Andreas to walk away from her, Isla thought bitterly. She remembered how he had snatched his mouth from hers when he'd kissed her at Stelios's house in London more than a year ago. His abrupt departure had left her wondering what she had done wrong.

Loukas gave a loud wail. 'Don't cry, baba,' she whispered, blinking away her own tears. Usually he was a contented baby but he had been restless during his feed and his yells broke her heart even more than Andreas had done. How idiotic she had been to hope that when he saw Loukas he would realise that the baby was his son. They looked so alike, but perhaps all babies looked the same and only their mothers saw every unique detail of their child's features, she thought. Loukas had even inherited his father's piercing blue eyes, but the cold rejection in Andreas's eyes would stay with Isla for ever.

Was this how her mother had felt when David Stanford had abandoned her and left her with a three-month-old baby? Isla refused to think of David as her father. He'd stuck around long enough to put his name on her birth certificate, but Andreas had not even done that for Loukas.

There was no point in feeling sorry for herself. She wiped her eyes with the edge of the baby's shawl and stood up to rock him in her arms. 'Don't cry,' she told Loukas again, her voice resolute this time. 'We'll be fine, you and me. We don't need anyone else.' A sob rose in her throat and she forced it back. She had grown up wishing that she knew her father and now her own child would have to do the same.

It had been a mistake to come here, Andreas brooded as he looked around the old fisherman's cottage. The cottage was his private retreat, but when he walked into the bedroom he was assailed by memories of the night a year ago when Isla had responded to him with a sensuality that had blown his mind.

It hadn't been his intention to make love to her when they had sheltered from the rain, but the chemistry between them had been as powerful as the electrical storm which had raged outside. He felt himself harden as he pictured her gorgeous naked body spread out on the sheets, the shy smile she'd given him when he'd positioned himself above her.

There was no question that she had been a virgin. He felt guilty even now, remembering the gasp of pain she'd made when he had thrust his shaft into her and met the fragile barrier of her innocence. But it had been too late to pull back and he had claimed her with a hunger he'd never felt so intensely with any other woman.

Andreas raked his hand through his hair until it stood on end. He was not a saint and he hadn't kept a tally of the number of women he'd had sex with in the past, but he always used protection and there had never been a problem. Sadie had said that the condom must have failed, but after she had publicly accused him of being her baby's father he had been given permission by a judge for a DNA test which had proved she was a liar.

Apart from Isla, the only other woman he had brought to the cottage was the wife of a Greek government minister, who had appreciated the privacy of the island. But his brief affair with Katerina had happened several years ago. Frowning, Andreas opened the bedside cabinet and picked up a box of condoms. He had been glad to find them in the drawer when he'd had sex with Isla. But now, as he checked the use-by date and saw it had expired two years ago, he realised that it *was* possible he was the baby's father. More than possible; it was highly likely. His gut instinct told him that Isla had spoken the truth when she'd insisted he was the only man she had been with.

Andreas swore. His life was spinning out of control and he did not know what to think or feel. He'd assumed that one day in the future he would make a suitable marriage and produce the next Karelis heir. But the idea that baby Loukas was his son, his flesh and blood, unleashed emotions that he'd buried deep within him for most of his life. Not least was the realisation that having a child with Isla meant that his life would be linked with hers for ever.

Like it or not, she was the mother of his heir. To say that he found the situation unsettling would be a laughable understatement, he thought grimly. Isla undermined everything he thought he knew about himself. The truth was that he hadn't wanted to accept that he could be her baby's father.

On his way back to the villa he passed the jetty and saw Dinos loading luggage onto the boat. The butler had a fear of flying in the helicopter. A brightly coloured bag caught Andreas's attention. 'I thought you and Toula were going to Athens for a few days, but you have enough cases for a month,' he joked.

Dinos grimaced. 'You know what women are like about clothes. Toula has packed four outfits for our son's wedding because she can't decide which one to wear. But the green suitcase and the striped bag belong to Miss Stanford. She asked if she and her baby could come on the boat with us over to the mainland.'

Andreas gave a nonchalant shrug to disguise his anger. 'You know how women change their minds. Miss Stanford has decided to stay on Louloudi. I'll carry her bags back to the house.' He glanced up at the grey clouds scudding across the sky. 'I suggest that you and Toula leave before the storm breaks.'

The baby was lying in the pram when Andreas strode into the villa. He did not know where Isla was, and he was too furious to care. If he hadn't returned from the cottage before Dinos and Toula had left on the boat, he would not have known until it was too late that Isla had gone, and taken his son with her.

His son. Andreas stood over the pram and felt a tightness in his chest when the baby fixed unblinking blue eyes on him. Eyes that were the same colour as his own. Everything inside him told him that Loukas was his baby. He closed his eyes and took a deep breath that hurt his chest. When he opened them again the baby's rosebud mouth curved into a smile and Andreas felt as though an arrow had pierced his heart.

Emotions ran riot inside him and the fiercest, overriding emotion was something he had thought he was incapable of feeling with any depth. Love. Instant and all-consuming. His knees felt weak and a lump formed in his throat.

Something powerfully possessive swept through Andreas, compelling him to slide his hands beneath the baby's small body and lift him out of the pram. He held him against his shoulder, marvelling at how tiny he was, how fragile and vulnerable. 'My son,' he said gruffly. '*Geia sou.* It means hello in Greek.'

His jaw hardened as he acknowledged the reality of the situation. He had a son who did not bear his name and who lived in England with his mother. But Loukas was half-Greek and he should grow up knowing how to speak the language of his father. More importantly, he would know that his father loved him.

Andreas's parents had not been demonstrative and when he was a boy he had longed for their affection, but his mother had seemed to dislike him and his father had been too busy to give him attention. By the time he was an adult he had dismissed the concept of love as an irrelevance and assured himself he had no need of such an unreliable emotion.

He touched the baby's hand and Loukas curled his tiny fingers around his forefinger. Andreas felt his heart swell until it seemed to fill his chest. 'That's right. Hold on tight,' he whispered to his son. 'I will never let you go.'

He glanced across the hall when he heard footsteps running down the stairs. Isla had changed into jeans and a pink T-shirt and her blonde hair was caught up in a loose knot on top of her head. Desire ran swift and hot through Andreas's veins as he noticed how the faded denim jeans clung to her pert derrière.

'What are you doing?' Her face was flushed and she hurried forwards, hands outstretched to take the baby from him. 'Was Loukas crying? I didn't hear him.'

'He wasn't crying. I picked him up so that I could introduce him to his father. It should have happened when he was born but, thanks to you, I have missed the first four months of his life,' Andreas bit out.

Isla's startled expression turned to puzzlement when she noticed her suitcase and the baby's bag that he'd brought back to the house. 'I thought Dinos had taken my bags to the boat. Your attack of conscience is too late, Andreas.' Her eyes glinted like polished steel. 'I've decided to leave with Dinos and Toula and take Loukas back to England.'

His gaze narrowed. 'You have to live on Louloudi for a month in order to claim your half-share, but if you fail to fulfil the terms of my father's will, the island will belong solely to me.' He made a derisive sound. 'Do you seriously expect me to believe you will walk away from a multi-million-pound fortune? What game are you playing now?'

'I'm not playing any game. I came back because Louloudi is Loukas's heritage and I had the idea that I could bring him here sometimes. But I won't risk him finding out when he is old enough to understand that you refused to accept him as your son. Of course the money would have been amazing. But I can work to support Loukas. Besides, wealth means nothing compared to love.'

'I agree,' Andreas said tautly. 'Our son deserves to grow up knowing that he is loved by, ideally, both his parents.'

'*Our* son? You have changed your tune,' Isla snapped.

Her anger surprised Andreas. He had expected her to be more conciliatory. *Theos*, she had stolen his son from him and he would never regain the first precious months of Loukas's life, he thought savagely. 'If you were certain Loukas was mine, why didn't you contact me when he was born? You had no right to keep him secret from me.'

'No right?' She glared at him. 'You forfeited any right to be involved with him when you wouldn't believe you were his father. You made the humiliating accusation that I'd slept with other men. Do you really think I'd have called you to announce his birth after the way you treated me?'

Loukas had fallen asleep and Andreas carefully laid him back in the pram. He pointed to the study. 'We'll go in there so that our voices don't wake the baby,' he told Isla.

After a moment she followed him into the room. He leaned his hip against the desk and ran his eyes over her, irritated to have to admit that it was not only anger simmering inside him.

Her slim figure belied the fact that she'd given birth a few months ago, and her T-shirt moulded the sweet curves of her breasts. He moved his gaze up to her face and glimpsed awareness in her eyes before her lashes swept down. It did not help his determination to resist her to know that she still wanted him.

'I was shocked when you told me you were pregnant,' he growled. 'It didn't seem possible that I could be responsible.'

She shook her head. 'I didn't want you to feel *responsible* for Loukas. All I hoped was that you would love him. Nothing else matters and material things aren't important,' she said fiercely. 'Loukas deserves a daddy who will read him a bedtime story, who will comfort him when he's scared and play football with him. More than anything, I hoped he would have a father who was better than my father—although it would be hard to be a worse one,' she muttered.

'You told me that your father wasn't around when you were growing up.'

'I know the name of the man whose genes I carry. His name is on my birth certificate and when I was a teenager I found him and told him that I was his daughter. But he didn't want to know me. In fact he threatened to take out a court injunction to stop me pestering him.'

It was difficult not to feel sympathy for Isla, Andreas conceded. Her story gave him a better understanding of why she had behaved the way she had. But nothing altered the fact that she had deliberately denied him the first four months of his son's life.

'When a pregnancy scan revealed that I was expecting a boy, I decided to change my name by deed poll from Stanford to my mother's name, Christie,' she said flatly. 'I didn't want my son to bear the name of his grandfather who he would never know, and he is Loukas Christie.'

'The fact that you'd changed your name would explain why you couldn't be found. My security team did everything to try to locate you.' He frowned. 'Why didn't you give Loukas my surname?'

'You were not present when I registered his birth and so your details are not on his birth certificate.'

'His birth certificate can be amended to include

me as his father, and his surname will be changed to Karelis.'

'No.' Isla walked across the room and stood in front of him, her eyes stormy. 'I don't want to have to explain to him that he has his father's name but there was no place for him in your life.'

'You won't have to do that because it's not going to happen,' Andreas said coolly. 'My son will have my family's name and he will grow up in Greece.'

Her eyes widened with shock. 'Loukas's life is in England with me. If you've decided that you want to have a relationship with him, then you can visit him. Maybe he could spend occasional weekends with you, or come to Greece for part of the school holidays when he is older. But while he is a baby he needs to be with his mother and I am taking him home.' She stepped away from Andreas and headed for the door. 'I must to go now. Dinos and Toula will be waiting for me.'

'They have already left Louloudi.'

She stopped dead and swung back round to face him. 'How do you know?'

'I told them that you had decided to remain on the island. A storm is forecast and Dinos agreed with me that they should go before the bad weather made the crossing to the mainland uncomfortable.'

Temper flashed in her eyes. 'I can't believe you lied to Dinos and Toula. I refuse to stay here. You will have to call your helicopter pilot and tell him to come and collect me.'

He shouldn't be enjoying this, but hell, Isla deserved to suffer a little after what she had done, Andreas thought grimly. 'I'll arrange for the helicopter to take you to Athens by all means,' he drawled. 'But Loukas stays here with me.'

Her jaw dropped and he pressed home his point. 'My son is a Karelis and he will want for nothing. You say that material things don't matter, but you know that is not entirely true. I can give him the kind of lifestyle that few people are fortunate enough to have. Security, luxury, the best education—and love.' He pre-empted the word forming on her lips. 'Make no mistake, I will love my son and I will be a good father to him.'

'This is ridiculous.' She marched back across the room and halted in front of him. 'You can't separate a four-month-old baby from his mother.'

'You're the one who wants to leave. I didn't say that you have to go.'

'I know what this is. It's about power, isn't it?' Isla jabbed her finger into his chest. 'You don't really want Loukas. You didn't even know he existed until an hour ago.'

'And whose fault is that?' Andreas gritted. 'You changed your name so that I couldn't find you.'

'I didn't…'

'If you had contacted me when my son was born, I would have been there instantly. You told me that Loukas almost died at birth, but even then you didn't give me the chance to be with him. But I have him now and I won't allow you to disappear with him again.'

'You can't keep me a prisoner here,' she yelled, and poked him in the chest again. Hard. The cool, composed Isla who Andreas had first met at his father's house in London had turned into the fiercely passionate woman who had given herself to him in the cottage. Now it was anger instead of desire blazing in her eyes, but when he captured her hand before she could jab her finger into his ribs for a third time he watched her pupils dilate and knew she was fighting her awareness of him.

He tugged on her hand, jerking her closer so that their bodies were almost touching and he could feel the heat between them. Their chemistry was a potent force, and a complication he could do without, Andreas thought darkly. It tested his willpower to resist the temptation to lower his head and claim her mouth with his. Her eyes widened and her tongue darted across her bottom lip. It did not make it easier to know that she wanted him with the same urgency that pulsed hard and hot in his blood.

With a choked sound she wrenched her hand out of his grasp. 'I hate you.' She flung the words at him before she marched out of the study. A few moments later, Andreas glanced out of the window and saw her pushing the pram down the path that led to the jetty. He let her go. She could not escape from the island, and when she returned to the villa he was going to tell her how things were going to play out from now on. It was time he took back control.

CHAPTER NINE

THE BOAT WAS no longer tied up next to the jetty. Isla hadn't really expected it to be, but she had clung to the faint hope that Andreas had lied when he'd said that Dinos and Toula had gone to the mainland without her.

It was Andreas's fault that she was stranded on Louloudi. How dare he make her his prisoner? But he wasn't as clever as he thought. She had travelled to the island by water taxi and had stored the boatman's number on her phone. All she had to do was call him and ask him to come and pick her and Loukas up and take them to Athens.

Isla looked up at the sullen clouds scudding across the sky. The sea was choppy and she didn't like the thought of taking the baby in a boat, but she couldn't stay on Louloudi when Andreas was threatening to keep Loukas in Greece. She was furious at his accusation that she had deprived him of his son.

It had occurred to her a few weeks after Loukas was born and they had both recovered from the traumatic birth that she should phone Andreas at his office—the only way she had of contacting him—to let him know he had a son. But the memory of his refusal to believe she had fallen pregnant by him, and his scornful suggestion that she'd had other lovers, had stopped her. She'd had enough rejection to last a lifetime and she was stunned that Andreas now appeared to accept Loukas was his son.

Her conscience reminded her that he had said he would love his child and he wanted to be a good father. If that was true, would it be better for Loukas's sake if his parents could set aside their hostility and negotiate how they could both be involved with their son? She gave a bitter laugh. Andreas hadn't sounded like he would negotiate when he'd insisted that Loukas would grow up in Greece. But if he thought she would hand over her baby to him, he was wrong. Her little son was all she had and she adored him. No one was going to take Loukas away from her.

Before she'd left the house she had hung her handbag on the handle of the pram, and now she searched through it and discovered that her phone and Loukas's passport were missing. Andreas must have taken them, and she was trapped on Louloudi. Trembling with rage, she pushed the pram along the track that wound around the island, not trusting herself to return to the villa while she felt like murdering him. She had reached the furthest point on Louloudi when a helicopter buzzed overhead.

Maybe Andreas had changed his mind and was going

to allow her to take Loukas to England, Isla thought hopefully. But another possibility made her go cold inside as she wondered if he intended to put her on the helicopter and send her away from her baby. She would fight him with every last breath in her body, she vowed.

To her surprise the helicopter rose into the sky and disappeared into the low clouds. A storm had threatened to break all afternoon and now raindrops stung her bare arms. She pulled up the pram's hood over Loukas and began to walk quickly in the direction of the villa. Her feet slipped on the loose stones and she stumbled and gave a cry as pain shot through her ankle.

Where were they? Andreas pushed a hand through his wet hair as he strode along the beach. Isla and the baby had been gone for hours and dusk was falling. Panic made his heart thud painfully hard in his chest. The wind drove the rain into his face, and the waves crashing onto the shore threw up sprays of white foam.

He retraced his steps and reached the path leading from the beach to the villa. Ahead of him he spotted Isla and he felt a combination of anger and relief. She was walking slowly and leaning heavily on the pram.

'Where the hell did you go?' he demanded when he caught up with her. She was soaked to the skin and her face was ashen. 'Why are you limping?'

She spoke with an effort. 'I tripped and I think I've sprained my ankle.'

They reached the house and Andreas manoeuvred

the pram up the steps and through the front door. Isla followed slowly and sank down onto a chair in the hall. She closed her eyes and her face was screwed up with pain. He looked at her feet and swore when he saw that her right ankle was twice the size of her left one.

'You need to take your shoe off before your foot and ankle swell even more,' he told her as he knelt down and untied the lace of her trainer.

'I can manage,' she muttered. He ignored her and gently eased the shoe off her foot, grimacing when she gasped and turned even whiter.

'I'll get some ice and you will have to keep your foot elevated until the swelling goes down. You might have broken a bone.'

'I'm sure it isn't broken.' She levered herself out of the chair and gave a sharp cry before sinking back down. 'Oh, *hell*. Loukas will wake up soon for a feed.' She ran a hand over her eyes. 'I wish I had never brought him to Louloudi. And I wish even more that I hadn't slept with you a year ago.'

'Are you saying that you wish you did not have Loukas?' An icy hand gripped Andreas's heart. He realised that he had only been concerned about how he felt to have a child, and he'd never considered that Isla might have resented her unplanned pregnancy. She seemed devoted to Loukas, but what if she stopped loving him? Andreas had spent his childhood desperate to win his mother's affection. He wanted his son to know that he was loved by both of his parents, but if Isla regretted sleeping with him, she might also regret the child who had been conceived as a result of their passion.

'Of course I don't regret having him,' Isla said fiercely. 'My baby is the best thing that has ever happened to me.' A shiver ran through her and Andreas forced his gaze away from the outline of her nipples jutting through her sodden T-shirt.

'I'm going to carry you upstairs so that you can change into dry clothes,' he explained when she made a violent sound of protest as he lifted her up into his arms. Her breath hissed between her teeth and he guessed she was in too much pain to argue. 'Loukas will be safe in the pram until I come back for him.'

She weighed next to nothing, he thought as he held her against his chest while he mounted the stairs. 'Why are you so slim? Have you been dieting? Wouldn't it be sensible to eat well so that you can feed the baby?'

Her eyes flashed silver with temper. 'Suddenly you are an expert on childcare? Have you ever tried to prepare and eat proper meals with one hand at the same time as holding a baby who cries whenever you lay him in his cot? Being a new parent is hard work, and being a single parent is even harder. But you wouldn't know about that because you weren't around to help when Loukas had colic and didn't sleep for more than an hour at a time.'

'You should have called me after he was born,' Andreas said tersely. His conscience pricked uncomfortably that Isla had struggled to cope on her own. But dammit, he *had* tried to find her after she'd told him she was pregnant.

'Why would I have called you so that you could insult me again?' She gave a bitter laugh that sounded more like a sob. 'I was too tired and sick to fight with you then. My friend Jess from the village in Suffolk where I used to live came and took me and Loukas back to stay with her on her farm. I don't know what I would have done without her kindness.'

Andreas's body clenched when Isla shifted in his arms and her breasts brushed against his chest. He felt the hard points of her nipples through his shirt and when he glanced at her face he saw a telltale pink stain run along her cheekbones. Damn this woman and the effect that her sensuality had on him, he thought grimly as he strode into her bedroom and through to the en suite bathroom. He placed her on a stool and opened the door of the shower cubicle.

'The quickest way to warm up is to have a hot shower. If you stand on your good leg and hold onto the towel rail, I'll help you take your jeans off.'

'I can manage. I'd rather die than let you undress me.'

He rested his gaze on her flushed face, and said sardonically, 'We both know that's a lie.' He hoped she did not notice that his fingers were unsteady as he fumbled with the button on her jeans.

'I'll do it.' She slapped his hands away and ran the zip down. But when she gingerly stood up she gave a gasp of pain and didn't stop him when he eased her jeans over her hips and pulled them down her legs.

The sight of her tiny black knickers evoked a throb of desire in Andreas's groin, and it tested his willpower to resist the urge to press his mouth against the lace panel between her legs. If there was a hell, he was surely destined to burn in its eternal fires, he thought grimly. Isla sat back down on the stool and he carefully tugged her jeans over her swollen ankle.

'Now your T-shirt.'

She shook her head. 'If you help me into the shower, I'll finish getting undressed in there. Will you go and get Loukas? He's probably awake by now.'

The baby had kicked off his blanket and he waved his chubby arms and legs in the air when he saw Andreas. He had heard other people speak of their hearts melting and now he discovered that it could really happen.

'Hello,' he said softly as he picked Loukas up and the baby snuggled into his neck. Andreas remembered the list Isla had recited of things that a father should do for his child. 'I am your Papa and I will read you bedtime stories and teach you to play football and take care of you when you are scared,' he told Loukas. He breathed in his evocative baby scent, as sweet as vanilla. When he held him against his shoulder, he felt the softness of the baby's downy dark hair against his chin. His son—but was he?

Doubt crept into Andreas's mind. Sadie's lies when she'd accused him of being her baby's father had driven a wedge deeper between him and his own father. 'You have brought shame on the Karelis family,' Stelios had told him. 'You were a fool not to get a paternity test done before your girlfriend sold a damaging story to the newspapers.'

He would not be a fool for a second time. A short while ago a helicopter had delivered a DNA testing kit to the island. Andreas laid Loukas back in the pram and pushed him into the study where he'd left the test kit. It was a simple, painless procedure to take a mouth swab from the baby and from himself. The samples would be collected and analysed and the result would confirm the truth of Loukas's parentage. Andreas felt a flash of guilt for doing the test without Isla's knowledge, but he had to know for certain that this baby who was making inroads on his heart was his son and heir.

Isla was sitting on the edge of the bed when he carried Loukas into her room. She had wrapped a towel around her and the idea that she was naked beneath it had a predictable effect on Andreas's libido. 'I don't have anything to wear because I packed all my clothes thinking I was leaving Louloudi with Dinos and Toula. My suitcase is still downstairs in the hall.'

'Wait a minute.' Andreas walked down the corridor to his own room and took a shirt from the wardrobe. 'You can wear this for now and I'll bring your case up later,' he said, handing her the shirt.

'Thank you.' She glared at him when he stood in front of her. 'Turn around while I put it on.'

Obediently, Andreas turned his back on her and was confronted with the view in the mirror of her naked, slender body as she unwrapped the towel. His mouth ran dry and he ignored the voice of his conscience that said he should close his eyes. He'd never professed to be a saint! Isla's hair fell damply around her shoulders and beads of moisture glistened on her breasts. He wanted to put his mouth there and taste her peachy perfection before trailing his lips lower to the cluster of gold curls between her legs. He gave a silent groan of disappointment when Isla slipped the shirt on and fastened the buttons. Andreas had almost forgotten the baby in his arms until Loukas gave a whimper.

'He's hungry,' Isla said. 'He usually has a bottle at this time but I haven't made up his formula milk. Give him to me and I'll feed him myself.'

He carefully placed the baby in Isla's arms and could not assimilate the feelings that poured through him as he watched his son feeding from his mother's breast. The two of them had had four months in which to form a bond, but Andreas had known his son for a few hours and he felt as though he was intruding on the special relationship that existed between a mother and her child. Every mother but his own, he thought, his mouth twisting. His mother had made it clear that she didn't love him and he'd assumed it was his fault, some failing on his part that made him unlovable.

He walked over to the window and moodily watched the rain lash the glass. For the first time in his life he did not know how to proceed. He was determined to keep his son with him but it was patently obvious that Loukas needed to be with his mother. Somehow he was going to have to persuade Isla that from now on her life would be in Greece, Andreas brooded.

'Why were you so adamant that I couldn't be expecting your child when I told you I was pregnant?'

He exhaled heavily. 'It seemed so improbable.' He considered telling Isla what had happened with Sadie. But he'd felt such an idiot when details of his private life had been headline news and the rumour mill had gone mad on social media. The fact that the story was untrue hadn't seemed to matter to the tabloid editors who fed like voracious sharks on the scandal.

'I didn't really believe I was having a baby until my first scan when I saw a tiny heartbeat. I have some pictures of Loukas on my phone, taken when he was a few days old in the neonatal unit.' Isla glared at Andreas when he turned away from the window. 'You stole my phone and Loukas's passport out of my bag. Can I have them back?'

'I have locked his passport in the safe,' he told her unapologetically. He took her phone out of his pocket and walked over to the bed to return it to her.

Isla touched the keypad and handed the phone to him. 'Because Loukas was preterm he was placed in an incubator at first, but when I was well enough, a nurse took me to see him and I was able to hold him.'

Scrolling through the pictures, Andreas felt a tight-

ness in his throat when he saw how tiny Loukas had
been, lying in a plastic incubator and wearing only a
nappy, with wires attached to his skinny little body.
There was a picture of Isla cradling him in her arms.
She looked pale and scared, and guilt clawed in Andreas's gut as he remembered her accusation that he'd
failed Loukas. The truth was that he had failed both
of them.

'You said that you have been staying with a friend
in England since Loukas was born. Don't you think it
would be better for him if you had a home where he
could grow up?'

'Of course it would. I have been looking for a place,
but my job is in London and properties in the city are
so expensive.'

He frowned. 'Who looks after him when you are
at work?'

'I'm on maternity leave and not due to go back to the
museum until Loukas is six months old.'

'What will you do with him then?'

She looked down at the baby and sighed. 'I suppose
he will go to a nursery. I was able to finish my PhD
while I was pregnant and I've been offered a full-time
position at the British Museum as an assistant curator.'

'Is that what you want, to leave Loukas all day long
while you go to work?'

'It's not ideal. I wish I could spend his first year with
him, but I'll have to work full-time hours and earn a
decent salary so that I can give Loukas a good stan-

dard of living.' Isla bit her lip. 'I meant it when I said I don't want the half-share of Louloudi which was left to me in Stelios's will. The island belongs to you and your family.'

'Loukas is my family.' Andreas's eyes narrowed. 'I have told you that my son will grow up in Greece. My apartment in Athens is not an ideal place for a child but I inherited the house where I lived as a boy. It is undergoing refurbishments and will be Loukas's home.'

Isla's face had turned almost as white as the pillows. 'Are you threatening to take my baby away from me? You denied he was yours, but now you are demanding that he will live in Greece with you.'

His jaw clenched. She looked so damned vulnerable and he hated that he was responsible for the fear in her eyes. 'I meant that you and Loukas will both move to Greece and we will all live together as a family. It will allow you to be a full-time mother to him for as long as you like, and there will be no need for you to get a job unless you want to return to your career in the future.'

The baby had finished his feed. Andreas watched Isla expertly hold Loukas against her shoulder while she pulled the shirt over her breast. She was so beautiful. Motherhood had made her softer somehow and even more desirable. He wanted his son, he reminded himself. That was the only reason why he was prepared to sacrifice his freedom. Isla had disappeared once, and he would not risk her taking Loukas away from him again.

She looked puzzled. 'Let me get this straight. You're asking me to live with you?'

'I'm asking you to marry me,' Andreas told her coolly. He ignored her shocked gasp. 'And I will take care of both of you.'

CHAPTER TEN

'YOU DON'T WANT to marry me,' Isla said flatly. She had no illusions that Andreas's proposal had been in any way romantic. But she was quickly discovering that his acceptance of his son had changed things irrevocably. She was glad that he wanted to play a part in Loukas's life but a loveless marriage was her idea of hell.

He did not deny it. 'I am determined to be fully involved with Loukas and it makes sense for us to marry so that we can provide him with the stability of growing up with both his parents.'

'We don't have to marry to do that. We can live independent lives and still be good parents.'

'How would that work, exactly? I have to live in Greece to run Karelis Corp. Would Loukas live in England with you one week and with me in Greece the next? It seems to me that he would spend much of his life on an aeroplane, being passed between us like a parcel. Does it sound ideal to you?'

'No, of course not.' She chewed her bottom lip. 'I

suppose I could move to Athens and look for a job, and you could see him whenever you wanted.'

Andreas shook his head. 'I am not going to be a remote figure like my father was when I was growing up. I'm already planning to cut down my working hours, and I *will* be there for Loukas every night to read to him and kiss him goodnight.'

Isla felt a lump in her throat. Hearing Andreas state his intention to be a hands-on father to Loukas touched her deeply. More than anything in the world she wanted her baby to have what she had never had—a daddy. Andreas had promised to love his son, to protect him and care for him. To her shame she even felt the tiniest bit jealous that Andreas would give those things freely to the baby but not to her. If she married him, he would tolerate her because she was the mother of his child, but he wouldn't love her. It was a shock to realise how much that hurt.

'It's a crazy idea,' she muttered. 'We don't even like one another.'

'We don't actually know each other very well.' For some reason Andreas was staring at her hair, which had dried in loose curls after her shower. 'Sexual chemistry drew us together,' he said bluntly. For the next month we both have to stay on Louloudi, and I suggest we call a truce. For our son's sake we should try to establish a cordial relationship. I don't want Loukas to grow up thinking that his parents hate each other, and I'm sure you don't want that either.'

She bit her lip. 'I don't hate you, but I won't marry you.'

'I am a very wealthy man. Think of the life I can give him, and you.'

'I don't care about money,' she said fiercely, remembering how Andreas had once accused her of being a gold-digger.

He nodded. 'I believe you. But this isn't about you or me. We need to do what is best for Loukas.'

Isla leaned her head against the pillows. Her ankle was throbbing and she felt mentally and physically exhausted. The storm was still raging outside and it was almost dark. Andreas switched on the lamps and crossed to the window to close the blinds. While she had showered he'd changed out of his wet clothes and he looked powerfully masculine in black jeans and a polo shirt. A little voice inside her head asked her why she didn't simply accept his marriage proposal and allow him to take away all her worries about how she would manage to be a working single mother.

Her eyes felt heavy and she forced them open. Loukas needed his nappy changed and a clean sleepsuit before she put him in his cot for the night. She gave a start when Andreas lifted the baby out of her arms.

'Does he sleep in there at night?' he asked, glancing at the travel cot.

'Yes, Toula uses the cot when her baby granddaughter comes to stay and she lent it to me for Loukas.'

'Tomorrow I will order nursery furniture and everything else he needs. But for tonight I'll put the cot in my dressing room and you can spend the night in my room with me.'

Her heart lurched. 'I will not.'

'You can't walk while your ankle is painful,' he reminded her patiently, 'and you certainly can't risk carrying Loukas. The obvious solution is for you and him to move into my suite so that I can help take care of him.'

'I appreciate that I'll need help until my stupid ankle is better,' Isla muttered, 'but we don't have to share a bed.'

'Are you worried that I will be unable to control my sexual urges if we are in the same bed?' Andreas's blue eyes darkened with anger. 'You have been trying to hide how much pain you're in but you are as white as a ghost. I am not so crass as to try to take advantage of you when you are at your most vulnerable.'

Now she felt guilty! Isla sighed heavily. 'All right, I suppose it makes sense,' she muttered. 'But only for tonight.' She looked at Andreas. He was cradling Loukas in his arms and the tender expression on his face as he stared at the baby tugged on her heartstrings. For the first time she really believed that Andreas intended to be a devoted father to his son, and in her opinion that was worth more than all the money in the world. He had said that they must do the best for Loukas. But how could a marriage between two people who mistrusted each other possibly work?

He turned his head towards her and their eyes met and held. If only Andreas wasn't the most beautiful man she had ever seen, Isla thought with a sigh. But the sense of connection she felt with him was in her imagination, she told herself. When he had made love to her a year ago she'd felt that they belonged together, but he had discarded her and made her feel that she was just another blonde who had briefly shared his bed.

With a sigh she concentrated on practical matters. 'Loukas needs a nappy change. Can you manage to do it?' She fully expected him to refuse to volunteer for such a mundane task, but he nodded.

'I'm sure I'll learn. I meant it when I said I want to be fully involved with him, and that includes changing his nappy.' Andreas smiled at her obvious surprise. 'Once Loukas has settled, I'll go and make dinner.'

Her brows lifted. 'I hadn't got you down as the domesticated type.'

'Careful, *moro mou*,' he said softly, 'or I will demand you return my shirt immediately.' The glitter in his eyes sent a frisson of sexual hunger through Isla. Her breasts felt heavy and when she glanced down she was embarrassed to see her nipples jutting beneath the shirt he had lent her.

'I'm curious,' she mumbled. 'Did your mother teach you to cook?'

'*Theos*, no!' His smile faded. 'My mother had an

army of servants to run around her and I doubt she ever set foot inside a kitchen. She wasn't interested in anything except her ill-health and her unhappiness, for which she blamed me.'

'Why did she blame you?'

'She suffered a stroke after I was born, brought on by a long and difficult labour. My mother never fully recovered, physically or mentally, from the trauma. When I was a small boy I had no idea why she seemed to detest me, but when I was older she never missed an opportunity to tell me that all her problems were my fault.'

'It sounds as though you had an unhappy childhood.' Isla imagined Andreas as a little boy, wondering why his mother seemed not to care for him. Loukas would never doubt how much she loved him, she promised herself.

'I was away at school a lot and I spent most of the holidays here on Louloudi with Toula and Dinos.' He shrugged. 'I learned to be independent and self-sufficient from an early age and those qualities helped me when I was starting out in my racing career. My father did not approve of me racing motorbikes and refused to give me financial backing, but it only made me more determined to succeed.'

It was not difficult to understand why Andreas seemed so emotionally guarded, Isla thought later that night. He had grown up feeling unloved by his mother. And his father's affair with her mother had meant that Stelios was often not around for his family.

With a sigh she checked Loukas on the baby monitor before she switched off the bedside lamp. Andreas had shut himself in his study, saying he needed to do a couple of hours' work on his laptop. Her ankle was turning an interesting shade of purple but the pain had settled to a dull throb and she hoped she would be more mobile tomorrow.

But first there was the night to get through. Andreas's bed was enormous but she wriggled over to the edge of the mattress so that when he came to bed he would know that she was only sharing it with him with extreme reluctance.

Who was she kidding? Isla asked herself ruefully. She only had to be in the same room with Andreas and her body went haywire, every cell, every nerve fiercely aware of him. Earlier he had carried her into the sitting room of his suite and sat her at the table before he served dinner.

'I'm impressed that you made moussaka,' she'd told him, thinking that her own culinary skills didn't extend much further than omelettes.

His grin had done strange things to her heart. 'I am not very domesticated. Toula prepared meals and left them in the fridge. I simply heated the food up.'

She had found herself smiling back at him and, although she only had half a glass of wine topped up with soda water, she felt relaxed yet at the same time more alive than she'd ever felt.

'Loukas looks like you when you both smile,' Andreas murmured.

'I think he looks more like you. He has your colouring and his eyes are the same deep blue as yours.'

'He has a mixture of our genes and he's bound to have a physical resemblance to both of us.'

'I suppose so.' Emotion had suddenly clogged her throat. Loukas wasn't just a baby; he was a link between her and Andreas that would last for their lifetimes. 'When you asked me to marry you, what kind of marriage were you suggesting?' She blushed and felt herself floundering. 'What I mean is, would you want a proper marriage?'

Andreas had given her a speculative look. 'By *proper* I assume you mean would we have a sexual relationship? Why not? We have already proved that we are sexually compatible.'

She was glad he hadn't pretended that he was in love with her, Isla assured herself. There was nothing romantic about Andreas's proposal and marriage was simply a way for them to bring up their son together—with added benefits.

Thinking about their sexual compatibility made her feel hot all over. For the past year she'd frequently had dreams of Andreas making love to her, but tonight, lying in his bed, those memories were sharper than ever before. Her nipples tingled as she remembered how he had caressed her breasts with his hands and mouth, and how he'd moved down her body, pressing hungry kisses over the sensitive skin of her inner thighs. Isla's breathing slowed and her eyelashes brushed her cheeks as sleep claimed her and she slipped into a delicious dream.

She woke with a start and opened her eyes. It was pitch-black and she could not see anything, but her other senses took over and she realised that the wind had died down and the only sound she could hear was Andreas's regular, deep breaths. She hadn't been aware that he had come to bed, or that at some point during the night she had moved across the mattress towards him. He was so close she could feel his warm breath on her cheek, and his male scent—an elusive mix of his sandalwood aftershave and something muskier and uniquely him—stirred a fierce longing low in her pelvis.

He was fast asleep. Now that her eyes were accustomed to the dark, she was able to study his face. His sculpted features were softened slightly and she glimpsed the boy he had once been, and imagined how Loukas would look when he grew up. Emotion tugged on her heart. She and Andreas had made a beautiful child together but they were separated by a chasm of mistrust. Except that right now the only thing separating them was the shirt he had lent her.

Her mind was still full of the dream she'd had about him. She could not resist touching him and felt the heat of his silken skin and the slight abrasion of his chest hairs beneath her palm. Closing her eyes, she imagined if they were a proper couple instead of almost strangers linked by a baby they had not planned to have. If they were lovers she could trace her fingertips over the hard ridges of his abdominal muscles and discover the indent of his navel, before following the arrowing of hairs across his flat stomach and down to where they disappeared beneath the waistband of his boxer shorts.

She froze when he stirred. But his chest rose and fell evenly and she released her breath and pressed her face against his shoulder. She couldn't resist kissing his satin-smooth skin. He tasted of salt on her tongue. If they were lovers she could slip her hand beneath the elastic waist of his boxers and trail her fingertips over a hair-roughened thigh. Her heart skipped a beat when she came up against his impressively hard, thick arousal. Before she could snatch her fingers away, he clamped his big hand over hers.

'Just so that there are no misunderstandings, *omorfia mou*, you were the one to take advantage of me,' he growled.

Isla stared at his face, so hard and angular with the skin pulled tight over his sharp cheekbones. His eyes gleamed with a predatory hunger that sent a quiver of response through her. 'I advise you not to start something unless you are prepared for me to finish it.'

Embarrassed heat scorched a path from Isla's face right down to her toes. 'I was having a dream,' she choked.

'I thought I must be dreaming when I felt you touching me but the reality is even better.' The lazy satisfaction in Andreas's voice and the gleam of triumph in his eyes made her feel sick with mortification.

What had she done? She had shown him that she was still desperate for him, despite the fact that he had never bothered to get in contact with her after the night she had spent with him. Sure, he had been busy trying to save Karelis Corp but he could have phoned her after she'd left Louloudi. He had told her he'd looked for her after she'd visited him in Athens to tell him she was pregnant, but she only had his word, Isla thought bleakly. The truth was that Andreas had viewed her as a sexual diversion. The chemistry between them was a bonus in a marriage that he had only suggested because he wanted his heir.

She sat up and pulled the sheet up to her chin. 'I don't want to have sex with you.'

'You could have fooled me,' he drawled. But his dry comment did not disguise the bite of frustration in his voice. 'I know you want me. Your body has been sending out signals from the moment we met each other again.' He ran his finger lightly down her cheek and then lower, skimming over her throat before slipping beneath the sheet and finding the hollow between her breasts.

She wondered if he could feel the frantic thud of her heart. In the darkness his eyes glittered like blue flames as he lowered his head until his mouth almost grazed hers. Almost, but not quite. Part of her wanted him to take control and kiss her. If he did, she would not be able to resist him. The hunger inside her craved his touch—his lips, his hands, his body driving into hers.

'Let me make love to you, *moro mou*.'

Temptation clawed in her stomach. It would be so easy to let him ease her loneliness. When she was in his arms she could pretend that he was offering more than sex. But afterwards he might walk away from her as he had done in the past, leaving her self-respect in tatters.

'No.' She shifted across the mattress away from him. 'Just because I had a dream doesn't mean that I want to get involved with you again. You are the father of my child, but we are practically strangers and the little bit I know of you I don't like very much. I'm won't be your convenient wife and provide sex on demand.'

'*Theos*, I would not make any demands on you,' Andreas ground out. 'When we have sex it will be because you are as willing and eager as you were when you gave your virginity to me. And note that I said *when*, not *if*. You will come to me, and I can wait.' He cursed when she swung her legs over the side of the bed and yelped as she tried to put weight on her injured foot. 'What are you doing?'

'I can't stay in your bed. I'll sleep on the sofa in your dressing room. At least I'll be nearer to Loukas if he wakes up.'

'Get back into bed,' Andreas said tersely. 'I'll take the sofa. Do not argue with me, Isla. You have already tested my control to its limits,' he told her as he strode into the adjoining room and closed the door with a thud that spoke volumes.

The next few days were difficult. Isla had felt thoroughly ashamed of her behaviour when she woke the next morning, alone in Andreas's huge bed, and recalled how she had touched his body while he slept. If she had woken in the night and found him caressing her, she would have accused him of taking advantage of her, she acknowledged on a fresh wave of embarrassment. She was aware that she was sending out mixed signals, and she felt silly and childish. She was a grown woman and a mother, but once again she was letting her past and her fear of rejection prevent her from satisfying her sexual needs with Andreas.

To her relief he did not mention what had happened—or not happened—she thought ruefully. She had expected him to make a mocking comment when he'd carried her downstairs and she'd stiffened in his arms and avoided his gaze. But he seemed to understand that her emotions were all over the place, and he kept their conversations to neutral topics, mainly about Loukas, so that Isla gradually began to relax.

By the third day the swelling on her ankle had reduced enough for her to be able to wear her shoes and she could hobble about, although Andreas always carried Loukas in case her ankle gave way. He continued to sleep in his dressing room, and in the morning when Loukas woke he brought the baby to her so that she could feed him. Those moments when they were all together and their son was at his most winsome made Isla wonder if she had been too hasty when she'd refused to marry Andreas. But he did not mention marriage again and her fear of rejection stopped her from asking him if his proposal had been serious.

Dinos and Toula arrived back on Louloudi, and a couple of days later Andreas said he had business meetings in Athens and left on the helicopter early in the morning. Isla missed him and she wondered how much longer they could continue to remain in limbo, with their desire for one another unfulfilled.

The day had dragged and her heart leapt when she heard the helicopter return. Toula had said that Andreas had asked for them to have dinner on the terrace, and the Greek woman was going to babysit.

'Loukas can spend the night at my house. I am used having my grandchildren to stay, and it will do you good to have an evening off,' Toula told Isla firmly. 'The baby will be fine with me, so stop worrying and enjoy some time with Andreas.' Her eyes twinkled and Isla didn't have the heart to explain that her relationship with Andreas was not the great romance that Toula clearly believed.

Nevertheless she felt a sense of anticipation when she took a silk wrap-around dress in soft green out of the wardrobe and slipped it on. The material felt sensual against her skin and the dress flattered her slim figure that she'd been lucky enough to regain quickly after giving birth to Loukas. She teamed the dress with strappy silver sandals and slid a chunky silver bracelet onto her wrist. Her hair had grown like crazy while she was pregnant and reached almost to her waist. She clipped the front sections back from her face, added a slick of rose-pink gloss to her lips and sprayed perfume to her pulse points.

Andreas was already outside on the terrace and Isla hesitated in the doorway and roamed her eyes over him. He looked incredibly sexy in black trousers and a black silk shirt, open at the throat to reveal a vee of olive skin and a sprinkling of his chest hairs.

He looked over at her, and as their eyes locked Isla glimpsed a predatory hunger in his gaze that made the weakness in her limbs so much worse. For a moment she allowed herself to imagine if this scene played out differently—if they had been a loving couple and devoted parents to their son. Andreas would ask if Loukas had settled, before he drew her into his arms and kissed her mouth—slow and sensual with a promise of the passion that would explode between them after dinner, when he would lead her up to their bedroom and make long, sweet love to her.

Longing for all that she could not have pierced like an arrow through her heart but she forced herself to smile. 'Are we celebrating something?' she murmured, eyeing the bottle of champagne in an ice bucket. There was a huge bouquet of flowers on the table and a few packages gift-wrapped in silver paper.

Andreas popped the cork on the champagne, filled
two glasses and offered her one. 'Happy birthday.'

She swallowed hard. 'How did you know that today
is my birthday?'

'I saw your date of birth in your passport. By the way,
I have put Loukas's passport in your bedside drawer.'

Isla buried her face in the mixed bouquet of pink
roses, white lilies and blue freesias. Their perfume was
heavenly. 'I haven't celebrated my birthday since Mum
died,' she said in a choked voice.

'No tears on your birthday.' Andreas brushed his thumb
over Isla's damp cheeks. He felt a tug in his chest when
she blinked and gave him a wobbly smile.

'I can't believe you bought me presents.'

'They're nothing much,' he said, feeling awkward.
He'd spent hours when he should have been at work,
walking around the shopping district in Athens and
wondering what to buy her. He'd never actually chosen
a gift for a woman before. That was something he left to
his PA to organise, and he had an account with an exclusive jeweller who provided something suitably sparkly
and expensive when he ended an affair with a mistress.

But Isla was different from any other woman he'd
known, and she seemed genuinely delighted when she
unwrapped a book on Greek mythology, a framed photo
of Loukas smiling and showing his first tooth, and lastly
a sky-blue topaz pendant suspended on a filigree silver
chain. The necklace hadn't been expensive but Isla gave

a gasp of delight as if it was the most valuable piece of jewellery in the world.

'I chose it because the pendant is the colour of Loukas's eyes,' Andreas explained as she lifted the necklace out of its box.

'And your eyes,' she murmured. She turned around and held her hair up so that he could fasten the chain around her neck. Andreas breathed in the floral fragrance of her perfume and his stomach clenched. He wanted to press his lips against her slender neck. Sexual tension had simmered between them since the night he'd been woken by her hands caressing him. How he hadn't lost it then, he did not know, but he had promised himself and Isla that he would wait until she was ready to make love with him.

It was not surprising that she was wary of him, he'd acknowledged as he'd tried to get comfortable on the sofa, which had not been designed for a man of his height. He had done nothing to earn her trust, but that needed to change because she was the mother of his son and he would do whatever it took to convince Isla that Loukas deserved the happy family life which neither of them had had when they were children.

'Thank you for the necklace and the other gifts. I love them.' Her smile stole his breath and Andreas felt a frisson of unease. He would not fall in love with her, he assured himself. He'd witnessed the damage and devastation wrought by love and its associated hopes and expectations. But he liked Isla and it was important to win her trust so that Loukas would grow up with two parents who were friends.

'Let's eat,' he said, holding out her chair for her to sit down. The starter was a *meze* platter with a selection of olives, cubes of feta cheese, wedges of pitta bread, hummus dip and stuffed grape leaves. Andreas wasn't hungry, at least not for food. Isla looked divine in her sexy, clingy dress and his body stirred as he imagined unwrapping the green silk to reveal her soft curves and those perfect breasts of hers. He took a gulp of champagne and said gruffly, 'Tell me what Loukas has done today.'

CHAPTER ELEVEN

THE SUNSET WAS spectacular. A kaleidoscope of pink, orange and gold that stained the sky and set the sea aflame. Dusk announced the first stars, pinpricks of silver against a purple backcloth, and, high above, a crescent moon dominated the heavens.

Isla glanced at her watch and was shocked to realise that she and Andreas had been talking for hours. Dinner had been followed by a decadent dessert of honey and rosewater *baklava,* accompanied by rich, dark coffee.

'Why did you study ancient Greek history?' he asked, sipping a glass of ouzo, which Isla had declined.

'So much of modern culture is influenced by ancient civilisations, and Greek literature, philosophy, astronomy and medicine still have a profound impact on our lives today. When I was sixteen I went on a school trip to Mycenae as part of a history project about the Bronze Age and I was hooked.'

'With your qualifications, I have no doubt that you will be able to continue your career in Greece.'

Isla could argue that she wanted to take Loukas to

live in England. But she knew she would be wasting her breath. Andreas was determined that his son would grow up in his homeland and more than anything she wanted Loukas to see his daddy every day.

'I would like to work when Loukas is older. But he is growing so fast and I don't want to miss a day of his development.' She bit her lip, feeling guilty that Andreas had missed his son's first few months. 'I was upset when you refused to accept that I was pregnant with your baby,' she said huskily. 'I thought you didn't want Loukas, like my father didn't want me.'

Andreas leaned across the table and his eyes held her gaze. 'Have I convinced you that I would give my life for Loukas? I am absolutely committed to being the best father that I can be.' Emotion deepened his voice as he said, 'I love my son and I will make sure he knows how precious he is.'

Andreas's promise was everything she had hoped for, Isla thought. Well, not quite everything, she amended when he stood up and held out his hand to draw her to her feet. He wrapped his fingers around hers and she was intoxicated by the warmth of his skin. The spicy scent of his aftershave filled her senses and she was so aware of him it *hurt*.

'We'll go inside if you're cold,' he said when a shiver ran though her.

'I don't want to go in yet. It's such a beautiful night.' She walked over to stand by the balustrade and stared across the garden to the sea glimmering in the moonlight. Not so long ago she would have hurried away from him, too afraid of the feelings he aroused in her to stay when he roamed his hungry gaze over her. But she was tired of being a coward. She knew he desired her and she ached to be in his arms and in his bed. 'I don't want this evening to end,' she whispered.

'Well, it doesn't have to end yet.' His smile made her heart beat so hard she could feel it slamming against her ribs. 'What would you like to do? Can I get you another drink?'

'I want you,' she said breathlessly before she lost her nerve.

His jaw clenched but he did not move towards her. 'If this is out of gratitude because I gave you a birthday present...'

'It's not.' She didn't know how to make him understand her need that made ache so terribly. With a moan of frustration she flung her arms around his neck and pulled his mouth down so that it was a whisper away from hers. 'Kiss me, *please*. I think I might die if you don't.'

'In that case,' he growled, before he angled his mouth over hers and kissed her with a devastating passion that rocked her to her soul. The heat inside her burst into flame and she pressed her body closer to his, trembling with excitement when she felt the hard proof of his arousal nudge her thigh.

Andreas roamed his hands over her and cupped one breast, rubbing his thumb pad across her swollen nipple so that it hardened even more and she gave a whimper of pleasure. It was a whole year since he had shown her what her body was capable of and a white-hot flame shot from her breasts down to the molten core of her femininity. 'You drive me insane,' he muttered against her mouth. The evidence of his desire was a potent force and when he claimed her lips again with a barely restrained savagery she felt exultant.

She had missed him. It was crazy because they had scarcely spent any time together a year ago. But he had lodged like a bur beneath her skin, a constant torment to her. When he lifted his mouth from hers, he was breathing hard and a nerve flickered in his cheek. His blue eyes had darkened and were almost black, gleaming with an unconcealed hunger that drove everything from Isla's mind but her desperation to throw herself into his fire and burn in the fierce passion promised by his kiss.

Driven by an age-old instinct that pulsed hot and heavy between her thighs, she put her hands on his shirt front and felt the scorching heat of his body through the silk. It wasn't enough and she tugged open the buttons and smoothed her palms over his naked chest, glorying in the satiny feel of his skin and the slight abrasion of his chest hairs.

The long scar running down his chest did not detract from his male beauty. His powerfully muscular body made her aware of her softer feminine curves. She shivered when he spread his fingers over her breast, a possessiveness in his touch that made her heart-rate quicken. The ache deep down in her pelvis became an insistent throb as he skimmed his other hand over her silk dress, burning a path across her skin as he moved down her stomach and thighs until he came to the mound of her sex and pressed his palm against her. The effect was explosive and she gasped and arched her hips towards his hand, desire pounding a heavy drum-beat through her veins.

He kissed her again, without tenderness. But she did not care. His mouth was everything and her lips fitted the shape of his so perfectly that she could convince herself they had been designed for each other. She answered his demands with demands of her own and felt a surge of triumph when he groaned.

It had been so long since he'd made love to her and she was desperate to feel his hard length inside her once more. He drew the strap of her dress over her shoulder and peeled the material away to bare her breast. Her nipples were ultra-sensitive and she moaned softly when he rolled the swollen peak between his fingers, sending starbursts of pleasure down to her feminine core where she was so wet and ready. For him. Only for him. The world tilted as he lifted her into his arms and carried her into the house.

Mine. The word pounded inside Andreas's head and a possessiveness that he hadn't known he was capable of feeling ran like wildfire through his veins. He'd been startled when Isla had unexpectedly launched herself at him. Her rather clumsy attempt to seduce him had been endearing. She might not have the sophistication of his previous lovers but her sensuality blew his mind. It was just desire, he assured himself. The hunger that clawed in his gut was a kind of madness after a year in which he hadn't done more than disinterestedly take another woman to dinner.

He carried her up the stairs and into his bedroom. 'Are you sure this is what you want?' he muttered when he set her down on her feet next to the bed. He captured her hand and held it against his chest where his heart was doing its best to escape. 'Feel what you do to me, *omorfia mou*. If I kiss you again there is a danger that I won't be able to stop.'

Her eyes shone as bright as the stars. 'I want to go to bed with you, Andreas,' she said softly.

Theos, he was shaking like a schoolboy on a first date. His usual panache had deserted him and he cursed beneath his breath as he fumbled with the tie on her dress. Finally he was able to unwrap the green silk from her body and he released his breath on a ragged sigh.

'You are so beautiful,' he said hoarsely. Her black bra was semi-transparent and her darker nipples were clearly visible. Moving his eyes lower, he felt his erection strain beneath his trousers as his greedy gaze settled on her sexy black thong. 'Did you choose your underwear for me?'

'Yes.' She gave him a shy smile and he felt a tightness in his chest. It was just sexual attraction that made him ache in a way he never had before, he told himself. How could it be anything else? Emotions played no part in what he wanted from Isla and all he felt for her was lust. Satisfied that he was in control of the situation, he removed her bra and could not stifle a groan of raw desire when he cupped her bare breasts in his palms.

A saint would find her irresistible, and Andreas knew that he had been damned a long time ago. He stripped off his clothes and his heart gave a kick when her eyes widened as she stared at his powerful erection. He needed to slow things down, but when he pulled her down with him onto the bed the silken glide of her skin against his made him catch his breath. Supporting his weight on his elbows, he looked into her eyes, which were smoky with passion.

'Do you have any idea how many nights I've dreamed of doing this?' he muttered, not caring that his admission might betray the urgency of his need for her. He kissed her mouth, teasing her lips apart with the tip of his tongue.

She tasted of honey and the sweet ardency of her response tugged a little on his heart and made him wish for something he could not begin to explain. He liked the low moans she made when he cradled her breast in his palm and rubbed his thumb pad across her nipple until it was stiff and hard, before he transferred his attention to her other breast. Her skin felt like satin as he trailed his lips over her flat stomach and down to the neat triangle of gold curls between her thighs.

'Andreas!' Her shocked gasp made him smile. 'I'm not sure…'

'Let me show you,' he said thickly, moving down the bed so that he was kneeling over her and gently pushed her legs apart. He took a moment to study her as she lay there, all flushed and pink with sexual warmth. When he had first met Isla at his father's house in London, a lifetime ago it seemed, he had wanted to shatter her cool composure, and the knowledge that he was about to do just that made his heart pound with anticipation.

With a low growl Andreas lowered his head and ran his tongue over her moist opening. She gave a whimper and threaded her fingers into his hair but did not try to pull him away. He slid his hands beneath her bottom and lifted her towards his mouth. The scent of her arousal was the sweetest perfume and he felt the throb of his painfully hard erection. But he ignored his urgency. This was about Isla and he was compelled to satisfy her needs before his own.

And so he pressed his mouth against her feminine core and licked his way inside her. He explored her with his tongue and heard her cries grow louder as she arched her hips and dug her nails into his shoulders. Finally he found the tight little nub of her clitoris and sucked it. The effect was explosive.

Isla shattered around him and the keening noise she made was the most erotic sound Andreas had ever heard. It evoked a wholly primitive response in him, a need to claim his woman. He took a condom from the bedside drawer and quickly sheathed himself. Isla's eyes were closed and her breaths came in fast pants. She lifted her lashes and stared at him, her passion-stunned gaze mixed with a vulnerability which mocked Andreas's belief that nothing existed in his chest but a hollow void.

He shoved the disturbing thought away and positioned himself over her. 'Tell me what you want,' he demanded.

Her lips curved into a sweet smile that made the hollowness inside him expand. 'You, Andreas. I want to feel you inside me.'

He closed his eyes to block out the image of her golden beauty, her slender, lithe body so ripe and ready for him. *Theos*, he was going to come before he'd even touched her. It had *never* happened to him before. Breathing hard, he somehow regained control of his libido and pressed the tip of his erection against her opening. She was slick and hot and he groaned as he slid deeper, forcing himself to take it slow as her internal muscles stretched to accommodate him.

It felt good. So, so good. He let out a ragged breath and thrust deep, heard her give a soft gasp as he withdrew a little way and then drove into her again. She matched his rhythm, lifting her hips to meet each hard stroke, while she clung to his shoulders and tipped her head back, giving him perfect access to her lips. He kissed her hungrily, the taste of her sweet breath filling his mouth and the delicate floral scent of her perfume assailing his senses until he could not say where he ended and she began. They moved together as one, their bodies in total accord in a timeless dance that quickly built to a crescendo.

It couldn't last. It was too intense and he knew he was losing control. Gritting his teeth, he increased his pace, each thrust faster and harder than the last, driving them both to the edge. He slipped his hand between them and rubbed his thumb over the sweet, tight heart of her. She bucked against him and sobbed his name, shuddering with the force of her orgasm. And only then did Andreas's control crack and he pressed his face into her neck and groaned as wave after wave of pleasure engulfed him.

A long time afterwards he rolled off her and lay on his back, shocked by how much he hated being separated from her. Alarm bells rang inside his head. It was just sex, he reminded himself. Amazing sex, it was true, but it did not mean anything to him. It never had and it never would. Did Isla understand that?

He wondered if she would cuddle up to him and he would have to tactfully extricate himself from the inherent danger of post-sex emotions—hers not his. He wasn't into the whole cuddling thing. But when he turned his head towards her, he discovered that she had moved across to her side of the mattress and was fast asleep.

Of course he was relieved that she wasn't the clingy, needy type, he told himself. But the thought that she was unmoved by their tumultuous passion which had blown his mind was unsettling. Cursing beneath his breath, he rolled onto his side, fighting his awareness of her, so close to him and yet a million miles away. The pale glimmer of dawn slipped through the slats in the blinds before he finally fell asleep.

Isla stretched luxuriantly as she woke from a deep sleep. Her body ached in unexpected places but it was not an unpleasant feeling. She opened her eyes and stared at the clock. Eight thirty! Loukas usually woke for a feed at around seven a.m. Her panic subsided when she remembered that the baby had stayed with Toula the previous night—so that she and Andreas could spend some time together!

She turned her head on the pillow and stared into his bright blue eyes. Her hand moved to her throat and she traced her finger over the topaz pendant he had given her on her birthday because the stone was the colour of their baby son's eyes. It had been such a thoughtful gesture but she must not read too much into the present or Andreas's devastating tenderness when he had made love to her so exquisitely, she told herself.

'You look serious this morning. Is that because you regret spending the night with me?'

Did he? Isla wondered. Andreas's expression was unreadable, and old habits meant that for a moment she was tempted to say that last night had been a mistake. If she rejected him first she wouldn't feel so bad if he said he regretted making love with her. But she hadn't been the only one to have come apart utterly. Passion had overwhelmed both of them and the groan Andreas had made as he'd climaxed inside her had sounded as though it had been ripped from his soul.

'I don't regret anything about last night,' she said honestly. She wondered if she'd imagined a look of relief that flashed in his eyes. He smiled and her heart skipped a beat.

'Good.' He kissed her mouth, slow and sweet but with the promise of more. 'Last night was incredible. You are incredible, *glykia mou*.' He knelt over her and caught her chin in his fingers to that she couldn't look away from him. 'Why did you have sex with me?'

Was he worried that she had fallen in love with him? The truth slammed into Isla like a speeding bullet aimed at her heart. Right back when she had been Stelios's housekeeper in London and Andreas had visited his father, she *had* felt an inexplicable connection with him. Love at first sight was something she'd thought only happened in romance films and novels. She *couldn't* be in love with Andreas, she told herself desperately. Her heart contracted as she was forced to accept the truth she had tried to deny. A harsher truth was that Andreas did not love her. But he desired her and he wanted them to bring up their son together.

She searched his hard-boned face for a hint of softness that might indicate he felt something for her other than desire, but there was none. 'I decided that you were right,' she said lightly, although it cost her to keep her wild emotions out of her voice. Andreas's brows lifted in silent query and she explained. 'We are sexually compatible and there seemed no point in denying that you turn me on.'

His eyes narrowed. 'That's the only reason?'

'What other reason could there be?' she countered. 'We both want to be full-time parents to Loukas, and we're good in bed. The sensible solution is for us to be together.'

Something flickered on his face that she could not define and, although he gave her one of his heart-melting smiles, his eyes were cool and guarded. 'It's good that you are so sensible,' he said drily.

He lowered his head so that his mouth was a whisper away from hers, but Isla held him off with her hands flat against his chest. She was afraid to make love with him when her emotions were on a knife-edge, scared of what she might reveal while they were as close physically as they could be.

The warmth of his body seeped into her, melting her resistance, and with a sigh she wound her arms around his neck and urged his mouth down on hers. She told herself she was imagining a tenderness in his kiss. At first his lips were warmly persuasive, teasing hers apart and encouraging her response, which she could not deny him. As always, passion exploded between them and the kiss became a ravishment of her senses. He trailed his mouth down her throat and along her collarbone, while she ran her fingers through the dark silk of his hair and arched her trembling body towards his in mute supplication.

Andreas muttered something in Greek as he knelt up and shaped her breasts, tested their weight and rubbed his thumb pads across her nipples until they were stiff and tingling.

'Touch me,' he said thickly, and she was happy to obey, running her hands over his powerful chest. But then he captured her hands in one of his and held them above her head while he kissed his way down her body. He pushed her legs apart, his warm breath stirring the cluster of curls at the junction of her thighs before he put his mouth on her and took her to the edge of insanity with his wickedly inventive tongue.

By the time he drove his bold erection deep inside her, Isla was still trying to catch her breath after he'd given her two shattering orgasms with his mouth and fingers. She loved the feel of him inside her, filling her, and she lifted her hips to welcome each hard thrust as he took her to the edge of the precipice yet again.

He paused and stared down at her, and she could not define the almost haunted expression that darkened his blue eyes. The air between them trembled with something fragile and ephemeral, and then Andreas pulled back and drove into her one last time, his harsh groan mingling with her cries of pleasure as they tumbled over the edge together.

CHAPTER TWELVE

THE HELICOPTER LANDED on Louloudi and Andreas climbed out and scanned the garden, hoping to see Isla walking across the lawn to meet him. There was no sign of her and his jaw clenched with disappointment. He had only been away for a few hours but he'd missed her.

The thought made him frown. Missing her suggested that he'd formed some sort of emotional bond with her, but that was a ridiculous idea. He separated the people in his life into distinct categories: family, friends, work associates and lovers. Isla fell somewhere between the first and the last. She was the mother of his child, although neither she nor his son bore his name. Yet to describe her as his mistress simply did not cover his fascination with her.

They had been living together on the island for almost three weeks and Andreas felt a contentment he'd never felt before. Karelis Corp was safe and its share price had continued to climb since the problems it had faced a year ago. He had the full support of his board and had proved he was a worthy successor to Stelios.

But he was determined not to allow work to dominate his life like his father had done and, although he went to his office in Athens most days, he returned to Louloudi every afternoon so that he could spend time with Loukas.

He thought about Isla all the time. He was addicted to her as if she were a narcotic in his blood, and he was fairly certain that she was as swept away by their passion as him. But, apart from her cries of pleasure every time he gave her an orgasm, she was otherwise coolly composed so that he had no idea what she was thinking, and it frustrated the hell out of him.

Holding the box which he had brought with him from Athens under his arm, he walked into the villa and checked the ground floor rooms before he went upstairs in search of Isla. Concern for her had been the reason why he had left work early. He strode across the sitting room of his private suite, halting in the doorway that led into the nursery.

Isla was rocking Loukas in her arms. Her eyes widened in surprise when she glanced over and saw Andreas but there was no welcoming smile on her lips. She placed the baby in the cot and walked towards him. His stomach clenched when he saw tears on her lashes.

'I suppose you've seen the awful things that are being said about me on social media?' She closed the nursery door and picked up her phone from the coffee table. 'Many of the tabloids printed a photo of us kissing. The picture must have been taken without our knowledge when you took me shopping in Athens last week. It was such a lovely day, but now this—' She thrust her phone at him.

Andreas did not need to look at the screen. He'd already seen the damning photograph, and he silently cursed the impulse that had come over him while they had been strolling through a park to pull her into his arms and kiss her. He never made a public spectacle of himself, but Isla had said something which had made him laugh, and when he'd looked at her lovely face he'd felt as though they were the only two people in the world.

He had given in to his urgent need to kiss her, forgetting that as the head of one of Greece's most prominent companies he was easily recognisable by the paparazzi. Evidently a journalist had also recognised that Isla had been Stelios Karelis's fiancée.

'The most popular story trending on social media platforms is that I am a gold-digger who had previously hooked up with your ageing father, and now I've turned my feminine wiles on you,' she said in a choked voice. 'I'm just glad that we left Loukas on Louloudi with Toula, and the media haven't found out that we have a baby.'

'But we can't keep him hidden for ever,' Andreas said quietly. Their privacy was protected while they remained on the island but it couldn't last. 'I haven't even told my sister that we have a baby. But I don't want a nosey journalist to find out about Loukas and write an exposé about our—' he made speech marks with his fingers '—"secret love child". We need to take control of the situation and issue a press statement to announce that we have a son. And…'

He hesitated and caught hold of her hands. As he stared at her, he was aware of an indefinable tugging sensation in his chest when he saw that her eyes were the colour of wet slate, glistening with tears.

There was only one option open to them that made sense. It was Loukas's right to grow up a Karelis and have the support and love of both his parents. Determination swept through Andreas. Over the past weeks he knew that he and Isla had become friends as well as lovers.

In truth, it had surprised him. He'd never before had a friendship with a woman. He got on well with female work colleagues and he usually parted on good terms with his mistresses. But essentially he was a man's man, and during the years that he'd raced motorbikes his friends had been mainly other bikers and engineers. The high testosterone atmosphere of the racing circuit hadn't given any opportunity for soul-searching conversations, he thought wryly.

Isla was intelligent with a dry sense of humour, and her passion for Greek history was something Andreas shared. He was proud of his homeland and glad that his son would learn about his heritage from both his parents. He and Isla could make a good life together, he brooded.

'And?' she prompted him.

He tightened his hold on her fingers. 'And at the press conference we will also announce our forthcoming marriage.'

A host of complicated emotions swept through Isla but above all she felt a sense of relief. Since Andreas had accepted that he was Loukas's father, and he'd proposed to her, he hadn't mentioned marriage again. She had wondered if he'd changed his mind, or if he had actually been relieved that she'd turned him down. The facts had not changed however, she reminded herself. They were only discussing marriage because Andreas felt duty-bound to marry her. Yet she could not help but feel pleased that he wanted the world to know Loukas was his son.

'Do you think a marriage without love would work?' she said slowly.

'I believe it has a better chance than a so-called love-match with all the expectations and often false promises people make when they mistake lust for love. But there will be love,' Andreas murmured, and Isla's heart skittered in her chest. 'We both love our son and want what is best for him. You grew up without your father and neither of my parents had much time for me. Surely the most important thing is for us to give Loukas the family life that we both longed for when we were children?' Andreas lifted her hands up to his mouth and brushed his lips over her knuckles. The feral gleam in his eyes set Isla's pulse racing. He never tried to hide his desire for her, and he only had to look at her to evoke an ache of longing in the pit of her stomach. But was it enough? Could a marriage based on white-hot sex and a desire to create a family for their son really succeed? If she didn't marry him the alternatives—custody arrangements for Loukas, alternate birthdays and Christmases, perhaps sharing him with a stepmother if Andreas married someone else—made her go cold.

'I have something for you.' He released her hands and picked up a large, flat box that he'd placed on the sofa.

Isla looked at him uncertainly. 'What is it?'

'Why don't you open it and see?' he said drily.

She recognised the logo of a well-known fashion designer on the lid of the box and remembered that on the recent shopping trip to Athens she had visited a boutique in Kolonaki, the famous fashion district in the city. Andreas had persuaded her to try on a few dresses but she had refused to allow him to buy her anything and insisted on paying for a gorgeous blue silk dress with her own credit card.

Isla opened the box and her heart gave a jolt when she glimpsed white lace beneath the froth of tissue paper. She was stunned into silence as she lifted the dress out of the box and held it up. It was the most exquisite wedding gown imaginable—pure white silk overlaid with delicate lace and embellished with tiny sparkling crystals. The bodice had a scooped neckline and the dress was fitted at the waist and hips before flaring dramatically in a fishtail style with a long train at the back.

'While you were trying on dresses the other day, I wandered into the designer's studio and saw this wedding dress which she had just finished creating. It is elegant and breathtakingly beautiful and I thought it would be the perfect dress for you,' Andreas said softly.

Isla swallowed. The dress was like something out of a fairy tale, the kind of dress that little girls dreamed they would wear when they married a prince. But little girls grew up and discovered that even handsome princes had flaws. She wouldn't let herself get carried away by an unashamedly romantic dress, she told herself firmly.

'I don't know what to say,' she murmured.

Andreas's eyes glittered as he took the dress from her and laid it over the back of the sofa. 'Say yes, *omorfia mou*.' He captured her chin between his fingers and tilted her face up to his. 'I won't take no for an answer. Why are you hesitating when you know in your heart that it is the right thing to do? The passion we share is unlike anything I have ever experienced.'

She had only ever experienced passion with Andreas and he was the only man she wanted or would ever want, but she had more sense than to tell him. 'What will happen if it burns out?' Isla asked the question that ate away at her soul. 'Will you take other lovers? Oh, I'm sure your affairs would be discreet, but would you expect me to turn a blind eye, or take lovers of my own?'

A nerve flickered in Andreas's cheek and a savage expression turned his eyes almost black. 'I don't suggest you try it, *moro mou*. I don't share what is mine.'

She should have been horrified by his outrageously possessive statement but Isla felt a deep sense of relief. Their relationship might be based on sex but she was secretly thrilled that Andreas had staked his claim on her. She reminded herself that she was a modern, independent woman. 'I'm not yours,' she whispered.

He snaked his arm around her waist and hauled her against him. 'Tell me that when you are lying beneath me, and I am inside you,' he growled. 'Tell me you are not mine when you scream my name and rake your nails down my back every time I make you come.'

His head swooped and he covered her lips with his and kissed her without mercy, without tenderness or gentleness. It felt as if he was branding her and she did not resist him. Instead she succumbed willingly to his mastery because the only place she wanted to be was in his arms, in his bed and in his life.

When at last he lifted his mouth from hers, they were both breathing hard. 'I am prepared to commit totally to our marriage,' he told her. 'I will expect you to do the same.'

It was a far cry from a declaration of love, but strangely she was reassured by his blunt words more than if he'd pretended to have feelings for her. She stared at his harshly handsome face and her heart turned over when he said intently, 'So what is your answer, Isla? You are the mother of my son. Will you also be my wife?'

She took a deep breath and prepared to leap from the mountaintop. 'Yes.'

'Have I told you how incredibly beautiful you look tonight?' Andreas's deep voice wrapped around Isla like a velvet cloak and helped to calm the butterflies that were leaping in her stomach.

She looked out of the car window and grimaced when she saw dozens of press photographers armed with cameras waiting on the pavement outside the Karelis Corp building in Athens. The party to celebrate the company's return to the top of the rankings of Greece's most successful businesses was *the* social event of the year and the paparazzi were out in force.

'The media have labelled me a scarlet woman so I thought I might as well dress the part,' she said wryly.

Her ballgown had come from the same fashion design house as her wedding dress and it was also made of silk overlaid with lace. But there the similarity between the two gowns ended. The red dress was overtly sexy. It was a halter-neck style and the chiffon top was semi-transparent at the front and left her back and shoulders bare. The long skirt had a side split that reached her mid-thigh. She was wearing more make-up than usual and her scarlet lipstick gave the illusion of self-confidence that she was far from feeling. But evidently she did not fool Andreas.

'Try to relax, *moro mou*,' he murmured as he picked up her hand and pressed his lips to the exquisite engagement ring—a rare and stunning round-cut blue diamond surrounded by white diamonds—that he had slipped onto her finger two days ago. 'I have already given a press statement explaining that our relationship began after my father's death, and I have told family members and close friends the truth—that your engagement to Stelios was a pretence so that he could hide the fact that he was terminally ill. At the party I will announce that we are engaged and soon to be married, and that we have a son.'

She bit her lip. 'But if the press find out Loukas's date of birth it will be obvious that we must have slept together while I was pretending to be Stelios's fiancée.'

Andreas shrugged. 'I won't give specific details. And I doubt anyone will care, certainly not the shareholders. They will be pleased that I have thrown off my playboy image and settled down to family life and produced an heir.'

The car stopped and the chauffeur jumped out and came to open the rear door. Andreas's words were a timely reminder to Isla of why he was marrying her. He had been so attentive since she had agreed to marry him that she'd almost started to believe he saw their marriage as more than a convenient arrangement which would give him his son.

She followed him out of the car, half blinded by the flashbulbs that went off around her. The photographers pressed forwards but Andreas's security guards kept them back. He put his arm around her waist, holding her close to him in a protective manner that made her foolish heart leap.

The opulent hospitality suite on the top floor of the building was packed with guests, all eager to glimpse the woman who had apparently captured the heart of Karelis Corp's notoriously commitment-phobic CEO. There were murmurs of surprise when Andreas introduced Isla as his soon-to-be wife and the mother of his baby son. But the news was well-received by everyone—with one exception.

Halfway through the evening, Andreas's sister followed Isla into the cloakroom, which happened to be empty. Nefeli launched straight into a verbal attack. 'I suppose you think you're clever to have trapped Andreas with a baby. God, it's the oldest trick in the book. But I've got news for you. The only reason he is prepared to marry you is so that he can regain control of Louloudi. You persuaded my father to leave you a half share of the island, but when my brother divorces you he will make sure you get nothing.'

Isla told herself that there was no truth in Nefeli's spiteful words. Andreas had mentioned that his sister was still struggling to accept Stelios's death and Isla knew from when she had lost her mum that grief was a dark place. She pinned a smile on her face when she returned to the party, but a few times during the evening she looked round to find Andreas's speculative gaze resting on her.

'Are you going to tell me what's wrong?' he said later when they walked into his penthouse apartment in the city. They had left Loukas behind on Louloudi in Toula's care. The Greek grandmother adored the baby and Isla was grateful for her advice and experience that she missed from her mum. Andreas crossed the sitting room and slid open the glass doors which led onto the balcony. It was a warm night, and a huge, bright moon hung like a silver disc above the Acropolis.

Isla followed him outside and stared at Greece's most iconic landmark, widely regarded as the most important ancient site in the Western world. She had been excited by the thought of living in Athens and perhaps working at the Acropolis museum when Loukas was older. But now she was full of doubts and stood twisting her engagement ring on her finger.

'If you don't like the ring you can choose a different one.'

Her eyes flew to Andreas. 'Oh, no, I love this one. I didn't even know there was such a thing as a blue diamond.'

'The clarity and intensity of colour is superior to a sapphire. I like how the stones reflect the light, like the sun sparkling on the Aegean Sea.'

She chewed her bottom lip. 'It's not the ring.'

'We could spend all night playing guessing games,

but I have something much more enjoyable in mind,' he murmured.

'If we didn't have Loukas you wouldn't have asked me to marry you…would you?'

He made an impatient sound. 'But we do have our son, and he is a very good reason for us to marry. What do you want me to say?' He raked his hair off his brow and stared at her, his eyes glittering with an emotion she could not define. And she was probably imagining it, Isla thought. Andreas did not do emotions.

Why did she give her heart to men who did not want her love? she asked herself bitterly. She had idolised her father when she was growing up, despite the fact that she'd never met him. He had been a heroic figure in her mind, but she had discovered that he was selfish and not worthy of the tears she'd cried when he had told her to stay out of his life.

'Your sister said that you are only marrying me as a way of regaining full ownership of Louloudi and then you intend to divorce me.'

Andreas swore. 'Nefeli is still upset but it does not excuse her lies. I will speak to her.' He moved to stand in front of Isla and ran his finger lightly down her cheek. 'It's true that I suggested marriage as a sensible solution to our situation.'

Hearing him say it, even though he had never pretended to have feelings for her, felt like a knife through her heart. Fortunately her pride kicked in and she lifted her chin. 'With the added advantage of hot sex,' she suggested drily.

'It's more than just good sex,' he said thoughtfully. 'I have enough experience to know that the chemistry between us, the passion, is different than with other women. It's…special.'

Special! The word wrapped around Isla's heart like a security blanket. She had learned enough about Andreas to know that he did not say things he didn't mean. If he thought that making love with her was special it gave her hope that over time his feelings for her might grow.

'And there will be no divorce.' His voice was resolute. 'There has never been a divorce in the Karelis family.'

'Perhaps it would have been better if your parents had divorced as the marriage made your mother unhappy.'

'She made herself unhappy because she loved my father and it became an unhealthy obsession.' Andreas's jaw tightened. 'But that won't happen with us,' he said in a hard voice that sounded as though he was warning her not to fall in love with him. He was too late, she thought heavily. But if she told him how she felt, it would put her in a vulnerable position. He might even decide not to marry her and instead seek custody of Loukas. She shivered and Andreas frowned.

'You are getting cold out here. Let's go inside and I'll warm you.' His eyes gleamed with sensual promise as he swept her up into his arms and carried her inside the penthouse. The master bedroom had floor to ceiling windows on three walls and the views over the city were spectacular, but Isla only had eyes for Andreas as he stripped off his shirt.

Heat radiated from his skin and he smelled divine. The only place she wanted to be was in his strong arms. She traced her finger over the long scar that ran down his chest, a legacy of the motorbike accident that had almost killed him. Life was precarious and uncertain but he was offering her a future with him and their baby son, who they both adored.

When he bent his head and claimed her mouth with his, she wrapped her arms around his neck and pressed herself closer to him so that she felt the erratic thud of his heart beating in time with her own. There was tenderness in his kiss tonight and something close to reverence in the way he undressed her slowly, trailing his lips over every inch of her skin that he exposed and paying homage to her breasts before he knelt between her thighs and pressed his mouth to the molten heart of her femininity.

By the time he tumbled them onto the bed and lifted her on top of him she was shaking with need, and even more shaken by the realisation that his hands were unsteady when he guided her down onto his hard length. She rocked her hips, taking him deeper inside her so that he filled her, completed her.

He cupped her bottom cheeks in his big hands as she arched above him. 'You will never find passion as intense as this with anyone else,' Andreas gritted. '*Esai dikos mou.*'

His words thundered through Isla's blood.

You are mine.

CHAPTER THIRTEEN

'Isla, wake up, *agapimenos*.' The deep voice, as rich and dark as bittersweet chocolate, roused Isla from a peaceful sleep. She stretched luxuriantly and opened her eyes to find Andreas leaning over her.

'You remind me of a sleepy kitten and I have the marks made by your sharp little claws on my back,' he teased softly.

She blushed and sat up, tugging the sheet over her breasts, although heaven knew it was too late for modesty, she thought as memories of their wild lovemaking the previous night surfaced in her mind. Her disappointment that Andreas was dressed must have shown on her face. He looked breathtaking in a dark grey suit and a silk shirt the exact shade of blue as his eyes, but she preferred him naked.

'If you carry on looking at me like that I will definitely be late for my flight to New York,' he drawled. At her faint frown, he murmured, 'I told you about my business trip last night but I don't think you were concentrating on what I was saying.' His sudden grin made him seem almost boyish and even more gorgeous.

No, she had been focused on what he was doing with his long fingers and wicked tongue. 'How long will you be away for?'

'Three days.' A gleam lit his eyes when she gave a faint sigh. 'Come with me? Toula won't mind looking after Loukas.'

Isla was startled by his invitation. 'But you will be working.'

'Only during the days, but we would have the evenings and nights to ourselves.'

She was tempted, especially when he dipped his head and covered her mouth with his in an achingly sensual kiss. When she parted her lips he groaned and tangled his tongue with hers.

'I don't want to leave Loukas for that long,' she muttered when a need for oxygen made them break apart. Did she imagine a look of regret in his eyes as he stood up?

'I'll cram three days of meetings into two days so that I can return home early,' Andreas said thickly. He glanced at his watch and cursed. On his way out of the bedroom he halted in the doorway and looked back at her. 'Will you miss me?'

She wanted to deny it but she was a hopeless liar. 'Maybe a bit,' she whispered.

He held her gaze for what seemed like eternity. 'I'll miss you too.'

It was just a figure of speech, Isla told herself after Andreas had gone. She doubted he would really miss her, but she was already counting the minutes until she saw him again. The penthouse felt empty without him. She showered and dressed and was about to walk outside to the helipad, where the pilot was waiting to fly her back to Louloudi, when her phone rang.

Andreas sounded tense. 'I'm at the airport, but I left in a hurry this morning and forgot my passport. You should find it on my desk, and I've sent a motorcycle courier to collect it.'

Isla went into his study. 'I can't see your passport on the desk.'

He swore. 'The maid has probably tidied up. Can you check in the drawers for it?'

She opened a drawer and sifted through some paperwork in case the passport had slipped between the pages. She was amused that Andreas was so untidy. It was an endearingly human trait in a man who she still found enigmatic. The headed notepaper on one document caught her attention: *DNA Assured*.

Her curiosity got the better of her and even though she felt guilty to read his private correspondence she quickly skimmed her eyes down the letter. Her heart slammed into her ribs and her confusion turned to shock when she realised that the letter was from a DNA testing clinic where Andreas had requested a paternity test. The letter was dated almost a month ago, when he had met his son for the first time. But clearly Andreas had suspected that Loukas wasn't his child.

'Isla, have you found it?' Andreas's voice jolted her out of her state of numb shock. She pulled open another drawer and saw his passport.

'Yes, it's here.' Heaven knew how she managed to keep her voice steady.

'Good. The courier will be there soon. I have another call that I need to take.' Andreas's brisk voice turned husky. 'Think of me while I'm away, *moro mou*.'

Oh, you bet I will, Isla thought grimly as her phone slipped out of her trembling fingers and she stared at the damning letter. I'll think what an absolute bastard you are, Andreas Karelis. The last paragraph of the letter from the DNA clinic explained that the result of the paternity test would be sent to Andreas in a sealed envelope, but because a sample from the child's mother had not been sent for testing the result might take longer than usual.

A wave of nausea swept over her and she collapsed onto the chair as the extent of his betrayal sank into her stunned brain. All the time that she and Andreas had spent together on Louloudi—becoming friends as well as lovers—he hadn't trusted her. That meant he either didn't believe she had been a virgin when she had slept with him at the fisherman's cottage, or that she'd had sex with another man, or men, after him.

Isla crumpled the letter in her fist and pressed her other hand against her mouth to hold back a sob. She was beyond hurt, but she was angry too. Fury bubbled up inside her. How dare Andreas go behind her back and have Loukas tested? She tried to think rationally. He seemed to genuinely adore the baby, which suggested that he *did* believe Loukas was his. And if he really had doubts, why had he asked her to marry him?

She remembered Nefeli's claim that Andreas was prepared to marry her because when she was his wife her assets would become his and he would regain full ownership of the island. And then there was the highly publicised photo of him kissing her. He needed to convince Karelis Corp's board and shareholders that he was a reformed playboy and so he had announced their engagement. Presumably he'd intended to call off their marriage if the paternity test showed he wasn't Loukas's father. But of course he was, and she would have married him unaware of his deceit.

What a fool she was. Isla covered her face with her hands as tears seeped from beneath her lashes. She had thought that they had grown closer in the past weeks but now she had proof that Andreas did not have any faith in her. She had accepted that he didn't love her, but she'd thought she had earned his trust. She deserved his trust, *dammit*. And she deserved his love. But he wasn't worthy of her love.

Her backbone stiffened and she choked back another sob, angrily brushing away her tears. It struck her that she had spent far too much of her life longing to be loved, first by her father and then by Andreas. But she was wasting her time. Andreas was cynical to his core. He had even gifted her an exquisite wedding dress, knowing that their future hung on the result of the paternity test he'd had done behind her back.

God, she *hated* him. But she loved him too, and she despised herself for her weakness. She couldn't marry him now, and she dared not risk seeing him again for fear that he would undermine her fragile defences with his charm and charisma, which she knew were fake.

An hour later the helicopter landed on Louloudi. Isla asked the pilot to wait while she collected Loukas and then they were to immediately return to Athens. She had booked tickets for her and the baby on a flight to London.

Loukas was asleep in the pram when she entered the villa, and she ran upstairs and quickly packed the clothes she had brought to Greece almost a month ago. In three days' time she was due to inherit the half-share of Louloudi left to her by Stelios, but only if she remained on the island. It was Loukas's birthright but it was a poisoned chalice and she was determined to sever all links with the name Karelis.

Her heart clenched at the thought of her little boy growing up without his father. Was she allowing her hurt pride to influence her decision to take Loukas away from Andreas? The thought pricked her conscience. For her son's sake perhaps she should stay and confront Andreas, and they would have to find another way to be parents to Loukas that didn't involve a farce of a marriage.

She opened the wardrobe and her throat ached with tears as she stared at her wedding dress that she would never wear. Andreas had chosen a white dress that symbolised purity but he suspected that she'd had other lovers besides him. Isla felt heartsick. It was the only way to describe the tearing pain in her chest at the loss of a dream that she had wanted so desperately. She squeezed her eyes shut but hot tears escaped and slid down her cheeks. It had been cruel of him to give her the beautiful dress and let her hope that fairy tales could come true. Why was she so weak that she loved a man who treated her feelings in such a cavalier way?

Anger and frustration with herself as much as with Andreas swirled black and rancid inside her. She opened the drawer in the dressing table and picked up a pair of scissors. Driven beyond reason, she slashed the dress with them. The scissors were small but sharp and the blades cut through the delicate lace easily. Isla made another cut and another, destroying the dress just like her hopes had been destroyed. Above the sound of the ripping material and her uneven breaths she heard Loukas crying. Sanity returned and she dropped the scissors, utterly horrified by what she had done. The destruction of the lovely dress that a seamstress had painstakingly sewn filled Isla with shame. Loving Andreas had turned her into someone she did not recognise, and she did not want to be the person she had become.

When she ran downstairs she found that Toula had picked Loukas up from the pram. The Greek woman looked troubled when she saw Isla's bags.

'I have to go back to England urgently,' Isla mumbled as she took the baby into her arms. Loukas stared at her with his big blue eyes that were so like his father's and gave an angelic smile that squeezed her heart.

'When will you come back?'

'I… I don't know,' she lied, aware that she would never return to Louloudi. Tears filled her eyes as she hugged Toula. When she and Loukas were on the helicopter and it took off, she watched the island grow smaller and smaller and felt her heart shatter into a thousand pieces.

In his hotel room in New York, Andreas sloshed bourbon into a glass and paced restlessly around the room, halting by the window which overlooked Times Square. Neon lights flashed and yellow taxis were bumper to bumper on the road below, but he wasn't interested in the view. Why the hell wasn't Isla answering her phone? He'd been in meetings all day and hadn't had a chance to call her until now. The time difference meant that it would be late at night in Greece, and maybe she was asleep. But something didn't feel right.

She had sounded strange when he'd phoned her from the airport to ask her to look for his passport. And after the party, when she'd asked if the only reason he wanted to marry her was because of Loukas and he'd agreed,

Isla had looked hurt and, more than that, she'd looked disappointed, as if he had failed her.

He swirled the amber liquid around in the glass. The truth was that he had failed her consistently. He knew she had doubts about marrying him but he'd steamrollered her into agreeing, telling her and himself that it was only because he wanted his son. Isla had seemed to accept the limitations he had put on their relationship, but he wondered if she wanted something other than the emotion-free zone that he had decreed their marriage would be.

His jaw clenched. Whatever it was that she wanted he was incapable of giving to her. He simply wasn't wired that way. And he didn't want to be, he reminded himself. He had decided when he was a boy that he would never be a hostage to his emotions like his mother had been for most of her wretchedly miserable life.

He lifted the glass to his lips and swallowed its contents, feeling the whisky's fire at the back of his throat. Isla would be all right, he assured himself. She would marry him because she wanted Loukas to have a better father than hers had been. And he would give her a good life, financial security and the opportunity to pursue her career. He wanted her to be happy but he wanted their relationship to be on his terms, he acknowledged.

His phone rang and his heart leapt, mocking his belief that he was emotionally detached. It must be Isla returning his calls. 'Toula?' Andreas's disappointment turned to foreboding when the Greek woman spoke.

'What do you mean, they've gone?' Dread settled like a heavy weight in the pit of his stomach. 'Where are Isla and Loukas?'

Toula sounded tearful. 'Isla said she was taking the baby to England. Andreas, you need to come back to Louloudi. There is something you must see.'

CHAPTER FOURTEEN

THE SUFFOLK FENS on a dank day towards the end of October were bleakly beautiful. Isla took a chance when the rain stopped for a while to take Loukas out in the pushchair that her friend Jess had lent her. The cottage where she had been staying since she'd left Greece ten days ago was a converted barn on Jess and her husband Tom's farm.

'Stay as long as you like,' Jess had told her. But Isla knew she needed to make plans for the future, find a job and a nursery for Loukas and start living again, instead of existing in the fog of despair that had settled over her. It didn't help that Loukas was unsettled. According to the baby book, he might be teething, but she sensed that he was missing Andreas as much as she was and guilt made her feel worse than ever.

As she walked up the lane leading to the cottage her heart gave a jolt when she saw an expensive-looking saloon car parked outside the house. Andreas had no idea of her whereabouts, she reminded herself. She watched

the driver's door open and panic surged through her
when he got out.

Despite everything he had done, despite hating his
guts, her eyes swept over him greedily, taking in his big,
dark figure dressed in black jeans and a black wool coat.
Taking a deep breath, she forced her feet to move forwards. When she drew nearer to him she was shocked
by how haggard he looked. He could never be anything
other than beautiful but there were deep grooves on either side of his mouth and several days' growth of black
stubble on his jaw. He looked like she felt—defeated.
But Isla reminded herself that Andreas was far too arrogant to know the meaning of defeat.

She reached the front gate and curled her fingers
around the key in her pocket, wondering what her
chances were of pushing the buggy up the path, un-
locking the door and getting herself and Loukas inside the cottage before Andreas stopped her. Unlikely,
she decided, her panic escalating. She did not fear him
but she didn't trust herself to be anywhere near him.
Already she could feel the betraying tightening of her
nipples when she breathed in the spicy tang of his aftershave as he walked towards her.

'What do you want?'

His eyes glittered with some of their old fire. 'You,
moro mou. Always you.'

He was too much. 'Go away,' she said thickly.

'You would deny me my son?' His voice tugged on
her emotions and she swallowed hard.

'Do you know for certain that Loukas is your son? I assume then that you have received the result of the DNA test. If you were any other man I might have thought that you had come to apologise, but no doubt you're here to issue demands or threats.' She could not hide her bitterness. 'That's more your style, isn't it, Andreas? How did you find me, anyway?'

'You mentioned that you had stayed at a friend's farm in Suffolk after Loukas was born. I would have been here sooner but it took my security team ten days to locate you.'

'Why did you bother?' She pushed the buggy up the garden path. Loukas had fallen asleep on the walk but he would wake soon and want his milk. She grimaced when she discovered Andreas was close behind her.

'I want to talk to you.' A nerve jumped in his cheek. 'Please,' he added gruffly.

He had the benefit of superior height and strength and could overpower her easily if he chose to. She affected a careless shrug. 'Fine, you can say what you have to and then leave.'

She parked the buggy in the hallway and left Loukas to finish his nap. Shrugging off her coat, she walked into the sitting room and threw another log into the wood-burning stove. The cottage was tiny and Andreas had to stoop to avoid hitting his head on the low ceiling beams. He had also removed his coat and his grey cashmere jumper was the colour of the stormy sky.

Pain tore through Isla. Andreas's autocratic features

gave no clue to his thoughts. He was a remote stranger and she wanted to weep for the closeness that she was sure she hadn't imagined between them on Louloudi.

'How dare you arrange a paternity test behind my back?' she said in a choked voice. 'I have never slept with any other man but you.'

His mouth gave an odd twist and he pulled an envelope out of his back pocket. 'This contains the result of the paternity test. As you can see, it is unopened. The laboratory's seal is unbroken.'

She stared at him as he walked over to the woodburner and wrapped the cloth around his hand before he opened the metal door. The crackle and hiss of the fire sounded loud in the silent room.

'Wait! What are you doing?' she cried as he threw the envelope into the flames. 'Don't you want to know if Loukas is your son?'

Maybe he didn't care. She could cope, just, with the knowledge that he did not want her, but it was agony to realise that he was rejecting his baby. She leapt forwards and tried to reach the letter but it was already blackened and curling at the edges as it caught light.

'Careful, you'll get burned.' Andreas grabbed her hand and pulled her away from the fire. 'I received the test result a couple of weeks ago but I didn't bother to open the letter and I shoved it in a drawer in my desk.' He turned her to face him and clasped her shoulders. 'I *know* Loukas is mine, just as I know that you have never given yourself to anyone but me.'

She shook her head, stunned by the urgency in his voice and the fierce intensity of his gaze. His eyes were almost black but the terrible devastation in his expression couldn't be real.

'If you believed me, why did you arrange the test? It can only be because you don't trust me. But why would you?' Her voice cracked. 'I mean nothing to you.'

'That's not true.' His jaw tensed at her look of disbelief. He released her and raked his hand through his hair. 'I forgot about the damned DNA test.'

'You *forgot* about it?'

'I knew Loukas was mine the instant I saw him. But three years ago an ex-lover told me she was pregnant with my baby. I knew she hadn't only slept with me, and I asked for a paternity test. Instead Sadie sold a story to the tabloids saying that I was the father of her child but I had refused to support her and the baby. You can imagine the headlines,' he said harshly. '*Billionaire refuses to pay for his baby's nappies* was just one example.'

Andreas exhaled heavily. 'By the time a legal ruling gave me permission to insist on a DNA test—which proved that Sadie had lied and her baby wasn't mine—the damage had been done. My father was furious that the scandal reflected badly on Karelis Corp. Soon after the story broke I nearly lost my life in a motorbike race. If I hadn't spent the next few months in Intensive Care I would have sued Sadie for defamation of my character.'

'But why did she lie to the newspapers?' Isla's mind was reeling from Andreas's revelation.

'Money, of course,' Andreas said grimly. 'She knew the baby wasn't mine but she sold the story for hundreds of thousands of pounds.'

'If you had told me about Sadie, I would have understood why you wanted proof that Loukas is yours.' She bit her lip. 'Your lack of trust was hurtful. I thought we were friends but when I read the letter from the DNA clinic it made me realise that our relationship was hopeless.'

Andreas spun away from her and walked over to stare out of the window, as if he wanted to avoid her gaze, Isla thought. Looking past his big, powerful frame, she saw the skeleton of the apple tree in the garden, its branches stripped of their last few leaves by the autumn gale. Despite the cheery fire in the sitting room, she shivered.

'I wanted you the second I saw you at my father's house in Kensington,' he said harshly. 'If I'm honest, I assumed the chemistry between us would fizzle out fairly quickly. No other woman has ever held my interest for long. And I reminded myself why I didn't want to get involved with you.'

He turned to face her, his eyes narrowing when she made a muffled sound that betrayed how badly he'd hurt her. 'As a boy I had watched my mother sink into depression and a crazy obsession that ultimately destroyed her because she was unable to win my father's love. I was determined not to repeat the mistakes of my parents' marriage in our relationship.'

Isla had thought he couldn't hurt her more than he already had, but she discovered she was wrong. 'You were worried that I might be unhappy like your mother was—because I loved you but you didn't feel the same way about me? God, Andreas,' she choked, 'do you enjoy humiliating me?'

He crossed the room in two strides and grabbed her by her shoulders, his fingers biting into her skin through her jumper. His eyes blazed in his tense face and his beautiful mouth twisted. 'No, *omorfia mou*. I was terrified that if I admitted to myself that I love you—knowing that you don't, that you can't possibly love me, just as no one else ever has—then I would face a lifetime of pain, yearning for something that would never be mine. Yearning for your heart,' he said thickly, in a voice so raw that Isla trembled.

'You sent me away,' she whispered. It still hurt to remember how cold he had been when she'd met him at his office in Athens and told him of her pregnancy.

He nodded. 'In the year that we were apart I convinced myself I'd dealt with my inexplicable fascination with you. But when I walked into the villa and saw a baby with blue eyes like mine, I lost it. You were the mother of my child and even more beautiful than my memories of you. Loukas gave me an excuse to force you back into my life.'

Isla swallowed. 'You didn't force me,' she said with

stark honesty, and watched a nerve flicker in Andreas's cheek. 'How many other women did you take to bed as a way of dealing with your alleged fascination with me?' she asked in a low voice.

'None.' He stared into her eyes, his own unguarded, and the fierce emotion she saw in his brilliant gaze made her heart miss a beat. 'You are the only woman I have ever made love to rather than have sex with, and I haven't been with anyone since you gave me your virginity. I told myself it was nothing more than amazing chemistry, but desire is only a tiny fraction of what I feel for you.'

Isla took a swift breath, afraid to believe what Andreas seemed to be saying. 'And what do you feel?' she whispered.

Silence stretched between them and disappointment crushed her. Fool, she told herself. 'If this is about Loukas, I won't stop you seeing him. He needs you and we can work out a way for you to be part of his life.'

Andreas closed his eyes and when he opened them again Isla was stunned to see that his lashes were wet. 'Your generosity after everything I have done wrong shames me. It's not Loukas. He is my son and of course I love him and want to be with him. But I was wrong to insist that you marry me when I could see that it wasn't what you wanted.'

'I didn't want a loveless marriage,' Isla agreed.

'What about a marriage filled with more love than you can imagine?' He dropped his hands from her shoulders and wrapped his fingers around hers. 'I found your engagement ring in the bedroom at the villa.'

She bit her lip, knowing he must have seen the ruined wedding dress. 'The ring and the dress made a mockery of all I had hoped for. I couldn't marry you after I found that you didn't trust me.'

'I'd trust you with my life.' He lifted her hands to his mouth and pressed his lips against her fingers. '*Theos*, when I discovered your ring and the damaged dress, I thought I had lost you for ever, and I knew it was no more than I deserved. I realised then that my life meant nothing without you. I had tried so hard not to love you because I am a coward,' he said with savage self-derision. 'What I should have done was try to win your love, and that is what I intend to spend the rest of my life doing, if you will let me.'

Isla's heart was pounding with a mixture of fear that she had misunderstood what Andreas seemed to be saying, and burgeoning hope. 'Why do you want to win me?' she asked shakily.

'Because I love you more than I believed it is possible to love. Because I can't bear the thought of living without you in my life.' He swallowed convulsively. 'I want to see your face on the pillow beside me when I wake every morning and hold you in my arms every night. You have my heart and my soul, *agapi mou*. And if you will give me a chance, I will spend the rest of my life proving that I am worthy of you. If you will love me just a little.'

Tears slipped down her cheeks and he kissed them away with such heartbreaking gentleness that she felt as though she would burst with happiness. 'I can't love you a little.' The sheer agony in Andreas's eyes made her continue quickly. 'My love for you is so huge that my heart overflows with it.'

She cradled his beloved face in her hands and reached up on her tiptoes to kiss his mouth. He allowed her to be in control of the kiss for a few moments before he groaned and wrapped his arms around her, hauling her up against his hard body and kissing her with a mastery and bone-shaking tenderness that convinced her his love would last for eternity, as her love for him would last to the end of days.

Their son's cries made them reluctantly break off the kiss. 'Loukas has bad timing,' Isla murmured ruefully as Andreas dropped his hand from her breast and she tugged her jumper down.

'There will be plenty of time for us, *kardia mou*. We have our whole lives to fill with love, laughter, family.' The baby stopped crying and they heard him gurgling happily. Andreas smiled at Isla, his love for her there to see on his handsome face and in his eyes as blue as the diamond ring that he pulled from his pocket and slid onto her finger. 'Will you marry me for no other reason than I love you more than anything in the world?'

She blinked away her tears of joy and smiled back at him. 'I will.'

EPILOGUE

THEY WERE MARRIED in the little white church on Louloudi. The December sky was a vivid blue and the sun was surprisingly warm, gleaming on Andreas's beloved Aegean Sea. Isla wore her wedding dress, which had been remade, and she carried a bouquet of white orchids and tiny blue freesias.

Loukas looked adorable in his navy blue outfit and smiled contentedly during the wedding ceremony, held in his Aunt Nefeli's arms and watched over by his honorary grandmother, Toula. Andreas's sister had quickly come round to the idea of her brother marrying Isla when she saw how happy he was, and she adored her little nephew.

Nefeli had been waiting outside the church when Isla arrived, escorted by a proud-looking Dinos. 'I want to apologise for the awful things I said to you,' the young Greek girl said ruefully.

'Why don't we start again, as friends as well as sisters-in-law?' Isla murmured.

'I've never seen my brother looking nervous,' Nefeli

told her. 'If he paces up and down the church much more he'll wear a hole in the floor. He loves you, you know.'

'I do know.' Isla was smiling as she walked down the aisle towards the man she loved with all her heart. Andreas looked breathtakingly handsome in a black tuxedo. No longer austere and remote, his expression softened as he waited for his bride to join him in front of the altar, and pride blazed in his blue eyes when they made their vows and the priest pronounced them husband and wife.

'Well, Kyria Karelis, you're stuck with me now,' he whispered in Isla's ear as they posed on the church steps for the photographer.

'For ever, my darling love,' she replied softly, lifting her face for his kiss.

The family's lawyer, John Sabanis, strolled over and handed them an envelope. 'Stelios asked me to give you this on your wedding day,' he said.

'But how on earth could he have known that we would get married?' Isla was puzzled as she looked at the wedding card Andreas had opened. He read out what Stelios had written.

To my dearest son Andreas and his beautiful wife Isla.

I knew the first time you met each other that you would fall in love, and on this day, the joyous occasion of your wedding, I wish you all the happiness that you both deserve.

'I wonder how your father guessed that we would fall for each other,' Isla mused later that night when she and Andreas were lying naked in each other's arms. He propped himself up on his elbow and bent his head to claim her mouth in a lingering kiss.

'Stelios was watching my expression when he introduced us in London and he saw what I couldn't hide.'

She tenderly stroked a lock of dark hair off her new husband's brow. 'What did he see?'

'The look of love,' Andreas told her softly. 'Always and for ever.'

* * * * *

If you were swept away by
Proof of Their Forbidden Night,
lose yourself in these other stories
by Chantelle Shaw!

Wed for His Secret Heir
The Virgin's Sicilian Protector
Reunited by a Shock Pregnancy
Wed for the Spaniard's Redemption

Available now!

WE HOPE YOU ENJOYED
THIS BOOK FROM
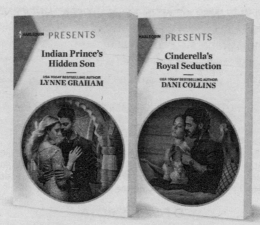

Escape to exotic locations where passion knows no bounds.

Welcome to the glamorous lives of royals and billionaires, where passion knows no bounds. Be swept into a world of luxury, wealth and exotic locations.

8 NEW BOOKS AVAILABLE EVERY MONTH!

HPHALO2020

COMING NEXT MONTH FROM

HARLEQUIN
PRESENTS

Available March 17, 2020

#3801 THE INNOCENT'S FORGOTTEN WEDDING
Passion in Paradise
by Lynne Graham
After a terrible car crash, Brooke can't remember her own name—much less her wedding day! So finding billionaire Lorenzo at her bedside—and a gold band on her finger—is completely shocking...

#3802 THE ITALIAN'S PREGNANT CINDERELLA
Passion in Paradise
by Caitlin Crews
Billionaire Cristiano can't get the unexpectedly innocent Julienne out of his head. He's sure another night together will cure him... until her bombshell destroys his fiercely controlled life! Because his onetime Cinderella is carrying the next Cassara heir...

#3803 KIDNAPPED FOR HIS ROYAL HEIR
Passion in Paradise
by Maya Blake
Determined to claim his child, Zak demands pregnant Violet meet him at the altar. And when she refuses? This powerful prince will keep Violet a willing captive on his private Caribbean island until she says, "I do!"

#3804 HIS GREEK WEDDING NIGHT DEBT
Passion in Paradise
by Michelle Smart
Theo has one goal: seeking vengeance on his runaway bride! Yet Theo can't escape their past...or the intense connection that spectacularly reignites. Will this tycoon be tempted to rewrite the rules of his revenge?

HPCNMRA0320

#3805 THE SPANIARD'S SURPRISE LOVE-CHILD
Passion in Paradise
by Kim Lawrence
Softhearted Gwen had always dreamed of the day tycoon Rio
would discover their child. Yet the reality is astounding! Because
when the brooding Spaniard sweeps back into her life, he
demands their daughter—and her!

#3806 MY SHOCKING MONTE CARLO CONFESSION
Passion in Paradise
by Heidi Rice
He's Monaco racing royalty and I, Belle Simpson, was his
housekeeper. But that evening, Alexi's searing gaze exhilarated
me. Five years later, I finally have the chance to reveal my secret—
Alexi's a father!

#3807 A BRIDE FIT FOR A PRINCE?
Passion in Paradise
by Susan Stephens
Samia's thrilled by the longing Prince Luca awakens within her
but knows a temporary fling is their only option. A future with him
is impossible. For the shadows of her past make Samia wholly
unsuitable...don't they?

#3808 A SCANDAL MADE IN LONDON
Passion in Paradise
by Lucy King
Kate is *mortified* when billionaire Theo discovers her secret dating
profile. Yet she can't resist his tantalizing offer to introduce her to
pleasure beyond her wildest imagination! But the biggest scandal
of all is yet to happen...

_____

**YOU CAN FIND MORE INFORMATION ON UPCOMING HARLEQUIN TITLES,
FREE EXCERPTS AND MORE AT HARLEQUIN.COM.**

HPCNMRB0320

*Theo has one goal: vengeance on his runaway bride,
Helena! But Theo can't escape the past...or the intense
connection that spectacularly reignites between them. Will
this tycoon be tempted to rewrite the rules of his revenge?*

*Read on for a sneak preview of
Michelle Smart's next story for Harlequin Presents*
His Greek Wedding Night Debt

Did she realize that every time she spoke to him, she tilted toward him? Did she realize that she fidgeted her way through every conversation? Was she aware that her breath hitched whenever he walked past her? Was she aware that at that very moment her hands trembled?

"The next thing I wanted to discuss is the kitchen," she said, moving the conversation on.

"What about it?" he asked lightly.

She tugged at the sheets of paper he'd placed his backside on. "You're sitting on my notes."

"My apologies." Sliding smoothly off the desk, he went and sat on the chair on the other side of her desk. "Is this better?" But she didn't respond. Her eyes were on his, wide and stark, her fidgety body suddenly frozen. "Helena?"

She blinked at the mention of her name and quickly looked down at her freed notes.

"Yes. The kitchen." Despite Helena's best efforts, her voice sounded all wrong.

It had been hard enough to breathe with Theo propped on her desk beside her—when he'd first perched himself there, she'd feared her heart would explode out of her chest—but when he'd moved off, she'd had to fist her hands to stop them from grabbing hold of him. Now he was sitting opposite her and she'd caught a sudden glimpse of his golden chest beneath the collar of his polo shirt, and in the breath of a moment her insides had turned to mush.

It shouldn't be like this, she thought despairingly. She'd spent three months under Theo's intoxicating spell, riding the roller coaster of her life.

He'd had the ability to make her forget everything that mattered. Under his spell she'd believed all she needed was Theo in her life to be happy. She was sure her mother had once believed the same thing before she'd sold her soul to a monster. Theo wasn't a monster like Helena's father, but his power over Helena had been just as strong.

How could she still react so strongly to him? She'd believed the sudden detonation of their relationship had killed her feelings for him, but she saw now that she'd been hiding them, hiding them so deep inside that she'd forgotten how powerful they were until one look at him in the Staffords boardroom had seen them poke their heads out from dormancy. Now the old feelings were slapping her in the face, taunting her, and it was getting harder and harder to fight them.

Eyes now determinedly fixed on the papers on her desk, she rubbed the nape of her neck, cleared her throat and tried again. "We need to discuss the kitchen's layout. Do you still want to consult a professional chef about it?"

She knew the moment she said it that she'd made a mistake.

Something sparked in his eyes. He leaned forward a little, a satisfied smile spreading over his face. "You do remember."

"Only that neither of us can cook." She quickly fixed her gaze back on her notes, aware her face was flaming with color.

"But you asked—specifically—if I still wanted to consult a chef about the kitchen… What else do you remember?"

She tucked her hair behind her ear and wrote something nonsensical on her notepad. "Have you a chef in mind to consult?"

"Answer my question."

Her hand was shaking too much to write anything else.

"Helena."

"What?" Helena intended for her one-syllable question to come out as a challenge. She might have succeeded if her voice hadn't cracked.

"Look at me," he commanded.

Heart thrashing wildly, she breathed deeply before slowly raising her face. "What?"

His voice dropped to a murmur. "What do you remember?"

Trapped in his stare, she found herself unable to lie. "Everything."

Don't miss
His Greek Wedding Night Debt
available April 2020 wherever
Harlequin Presents books and ebooks are sold.

Harlequin.com

HPEXP0320